THE RULES OF PLAY

ALSO BY THE AUTHOR

Days and Nights in W12

• P O E T R Y •

The Very Man
Paleface
The Age of Cardboard and String

JENNIE WALKER

THE
RULES
OF
PLAY

SOHO

First published in Great Britain as "24 for 3"
by CB Editions, 2007

Published in Great Britain by Bloomsbury Publishing in 2008

Published in the United States in 2010 by

Soho Press, Inc.
853 Broadway
New York, NY 10003

Extract from Chekov's *Sakhalin Island*, Oneworld Classics,
2007, reproduced with permission.

Library of Congress Cataloging-in-Publication Data

Walker, Jennie, 1951-
  [24 for 3]
  The rules of play / Jennie Walker.
      p. cm.
  Originally published as: 24 for 3. London : Bloomsbury, 2008.
  ISBN 978-1-56947-625-3 (hardcover)
  1. Test matches (Cricket)—England—Fiction. 2. Triangles
(Interpersonal relations)—Fiction. I. Title.
  PR6052.O9196A12 2010
  823.92—dc22
                                        2009031242

10   9   8   7   6   5   4   3   2   1

For Catherine

THE RULES OF PLAY

Friday | Saturday | Sunday | Monday | Tuesday

'*F*ive *days*?'

All I've done is walk back into the bedroom and ask who is winning. He tells me to lie down. He tells me that this is a natural question but not the right one. Today is Friday, the match lasts until Tuesday evening, they've been playing for only two hours and no one can tell right now who is winning. But England are doing pretty well, considering their injury problems. He asks if I'd rather make love for ninety minutes or for five days.

The players troop off the field to have lunch. None of them looks injured to me, they aren't limping or on crutches. He switches off the TV and looks at me, gathering himself.

'The latter,' I say, then think what this means. 'Is there time out for sleeping? Eating?'

'And shitting,' he says. 'But these breaks, they aren't long.'

'Reading?'

'Only aloud. A pleasure shared.'

'Then yes, the latter.' This is a different time-scale than I had imagined.

'Good,' he says. 'I feel that way too.'

He tells me it's a game involving many different skills and a lot of patience. Although there are times when outright aggression is exactly the right attitude. He tells me it can be affected by external factors: the weather, for instance, and not just when it rains—if there's moisture in the atmosphere the ball comes through the air in different ways, it swings or turns and the bowler can more easily deceive the batter. Or the condition of the ground, whether it's hard or soft or downright muddy. Or personal rivalries. Or delays on the Tube, or which side of the bed. Experience is good, but sometimes the rookies can do better than the older ones. They have nothing to lose.

'I have a lot to lose.'

'Don't let it change the way you play.'

'That's going to be hard.'

'Why else would you be here?'

I gasp, because he has just touched me exactly where

I didn't know I was wanting him to. Then he moves away, to leave me guessing where next.

It's a team game, he tells me. Every player has others with them, people they either like or don't like but they're there, in the team, and they depend on one another. Although often the whole game is changed by an individual performance. A lot of decisions have to be made, both considered ones, after weighing the pros and cons, and ones for which you have less than an instant of time, a blink of an eyelid. Mistakes are made. Not infrequently, the players feel that the game is unfair.

'Like life,' I say, pointlessly.

He shakes his head. At least, I think he does. Because we're lying side by side and speaking to the ceiling, I can't see, but there's a movement of the pillow, a tiny change of atmospheric pressure.

'Life is life,' he says. 'Cricket's only a game.'

'So tell me the rules.'

'No.'

'Why not?'

'Because I doubt that explaining things does any good.'

He sounds defensive, which is interesting. 'You're just being lazy.'

'No. Explanations always make things more complicated than they really are. They get in the way.'

'You mean, *seem* more complicated than they are.' Such a good time, after making love, to worry about definitions, when they don't matter a bit. A fuck.

'Perhaps.'

'And if you know the rules and I don't, how can I—'

'You wouldn't explain a joke, would you? It would kill it.'

'Is cricket a joke?'

'Depends how you tell it.'

'A long one. You have to wait five days for the punchline.'

'It isn't a joke. But nor is love. Explanations are pointless.'

We consider this, separately and together, looking up at the ceiling.

Then he says, 'Isn't mystery better? Not knowing all the answers?'

'That's a cheap line.' I slap him, harder than I'd intended, somewhere on his chest. 'At least tell me who's playing?'

'England are bowling, India are batting. According to the betting shops, India will probably win.'

For all the time I have lived in England, during my

so-called adult life, it seems that the English have been losing. And yet they go into each game with such gleeful enthusiasm, wagging their tails.

'And who are the two people wearing coats who stand very still?'

The odd couple: a bloated red-faced one and a small, wiry, dark-skinned one. These are the umpires, he tells me. When no one can agree about anything—whether the sky is too dark or the rain is too heavy, whether the ball is round or not round, whether a man is dead or still alive—the umpires decide. They know all the rules. They know more rules than are in the book. They stop any cheating. The bloated one is wearing a white hat with a wide brim that would look good at a wedding.

THIS IS MY lover who is speaking, my lover of only three months and one week so I am happy to listen to whatever he is saying, for the sound of his voice.

I interrupt him only to keep him going, to give him something to work with. His voice is steady and calm and lovely but not rational at all. Anything could come next.

'82 for 3,' he says. 'Not a bad morning.'

For me too it was good. Every part of me, inside and out, has been alive, and still is. His fingers are drifting on my skin, a lazy whisper. He's left-handed. His right hand is tucked somewhere between us, useless, for now. He doesn't know my body as well as, hasn't known it for so long as, for example, my husband. Not that *long* equals *well*, but that's the convention and he observes the conventions, watchfully, politely, with those very light fingers. You could say that given what we now know about each other, and what we've done to each other, politeness is superfluous, but I disagree.

He doesn't sweat and mine has dried on me, still there, a film. Inner thighs, teasing, flat of my belly and he wants me to turn over, I know he does, his right hand is coming into play, but right now seems too soon. Later—the luxury of that. Either that or I'm testing his want: it *is* a game, isn't it?

'I thought this was supposed to be one of the breaks,' I say.

I get up from the bed and walk to the window. This is a mansion flat, on the fourth floor, above the height of the trees that separate this building from the similar adjacent one, so I have to stand to one side of the window and look aslant to see any greenery, any other life. There is nothing outside to hold my interest, and nothing in this bedroom too, other than that man on the bed, and we both know it. Striped wallpaper, pale mauve, a small candelabra, fitted cupboards, the TV balanced on a chair.

Beyond, in the large living room, there is more to distract: books, on the shelves and in piles around his desk, and photographs on the wall of people at table or posed at some formal gathering; no special or repeated woman's face, I have looked. And she would, by now, have been spoken of, if relevant. Except for the books on the floor the whole flat is impersonal, male, slightly dusty; like a hotel room that the cleaners haven't been allowed into for two weeks. *Do Not Disturb* on the door. It belongs in a certain tradition: I have been, in company, in places like this before, without ever undressing or staying beyond dinner.

And it's unheated, naturally. I come back to the bed.

He wants me to stay for the afternoon session but I have to go.

It's me that's cheating.

I have very little knowledge of tradition, other than that it comes from a Latin word meaning 'surrender,' and even less of the rules, but I adore this man.

I stay for the afternoon session.

WHEN I GET home Alan is in the kitchen wearing his best apron, the one with stripes, like butchers used to wear and some still do, and just for a moment, as I stand in the kitchen doorway, that's how I see him—legs splayed, right arm holding a cleaver at shoulder height, about to bring down the blade on a hapless chunk of raw meat.

But no, dicing vegetables and measuring a teaspoonful of this and half one of that is more Alan's style. He's got his reading glasses on and a recipe book propped against the radio.

'I hope you're feeling hungry,' he says.

I suggest that maybe his apron needs a wash, and he looks at me over his glasses to assess my mood. It wasn't generous, what I said.

'How do you spell fuchsia?' asks Agnieszka, sitting at the kitchen table with a crossword and a shiny gold pen.

'F—u—s—c—h—i—a,' says Alan.

He's got the *s* in the wrong place, I think. It's not worth correcting. On the other hand, Agnieszka trusts him on things like this, and it could mess up her whole crossword. On the third hand, with a name like hers you'd think she'd be good at spelling.

Why am I in this mood? This day has been to die for. 'Where's Selwyn?' I ask.

'It's not as hard as it seems,' Alan says. 'It never is. Fuss-cha.'

Crosswords are recent. Agnieszka does them with Harvey, her new boyfriend, or friend. He buys the

Telegraph and uses the photocopier at the college to make a copy of the crossword, which she brings home. He claims it's good for her English. Harvey she hasn't yet brought home, or I'd have known. She introduced me to him last week, when I met them in the street, another odd couple. He's a shambling, awkward giant who moves with extreme caution, to avoid knocking things over. He has receding hair and wears highly polished brown shoes. He lives with his mother. He sucks mints. He has difficulty with making eye contact. He is both a child and in late middle-age. He's twenty-five years old and has been, maybe still is, married—this seemed unlikely to Agnieszka when he told her, but on the other hand she doesn't think he's a person who makes things up. He's honest, and he's kind. When he went with Agnieszka to a party he brought along a dozen cans of soup—he had a lifetime's supply of soup, he said, twelve cans was nothing. So maybe he does make things up.

'You don't like Harvey, do you?' Agnieszka asked me later that day. Each new boyfriend she offers to me, as a cat would a mouse, and every time I have to resist the impulse to pick him up by his tail and throw him over the fence.

'I do like him. He's very . . . '

'English!'

'Yes, I suppose. English. 1950s, maybe.' When I think of him I see him in black and white, not color. He doesn't eat enough fruit.

'Old-fashioned, yes, he opens the door. And he is very kind, always giving me things. And with Harvey, my English too is better.'

As though being good at English is something you pass on, like a disease. Something that rubs off, skin to skin. She's probably right.

'Agnieszka,' I told her, 'there's nothing wrong with your English. If you like him, fine, but you shouldn't be spending time with him just to get free English lessons.'

'No, no, it's not good. I have problem with tenses, especially conditional tenses, he noticed this. *If* clauses.'

'It's perfect, Agnieszka.'

She looked puzzled.

'I mean, for you. For who you are. Look, you've been here how many years?—nine, ten?—and you've found your voice, the English you speak is you. Some vocab, maybe. But really if you stay here another ten years—'

'Find husband, a dog, perhaps children—'

'A job?'

'A *dog*. You see?'

'This is how you'll still be speaking. Grandchildren, even.'

Utter dismay. 'I have reached my peak?'

She's twenty-seven. She is lovely. Except that she should have better than Harvey, I was making a mess of this.

Shocked, hurt, she made a pose like a woman in a Communist poster. The future, the five-year plan.

'I don't think so,' she said, very proud.

Now ALAN IS putting a dish in the oven. 'Forty-five minutes,' he says, looking at his watch. He takes off his apron, hangs it on the back of the door, and heads for the living room. 'Seven-fifteen, the highlights. You two stay and natter. It'll be ready at eight.'

'Highlights?' says Agnieszka, puzzled, wondering why Alan wants to watch a programme about hairdressing.

'The cricket,' says Alan, turning on the TV. 'First day. India all out for only 198 and we're already 64 for 1. That's a lot of wickets for the first day. England are doing pretty well.' He's almost rubbing his hands. I can smell the garlic.

'Despite their injury problems.'

He stares at me, amazed.

Agnieszka, recognising a tone in my voice that makes her uneasy, says she's got homework and scuttles upstairs.

JENNIE WALKER

'Do you know where Selwyn is?' I ask as she disappears. I shrug, and sit beside Alan on the sofa.

What we are watching is a foreign film, without subtitles. I remind myself that I should not be trying to work out who is winning, because that is not the right question, but even so the storyline seems jerky and lacking any realistic motivation. Perhaps because this is the abridged version. The ball is flung at high speed towards the batter, who either hits it or misses it, and occasionally everyone leaps in the air and one of the umpires either pretends he hasn't noticed or makes a rude gesture towards the batter.

'He's not going to stop it now,' says the commentator. 'The ball goes over the rope and that's four runs. Vaughan will have to think about posting a third man.' Idiot. He must be blind. There already is a third man: it's Selwyn.

After fifteen minutes there is a break for ads and I turn towards Alan.

'Tell me,' I say to him quietly, 'what is happening.'

Alan's eyes swivel from front to side and back to the screen.

'I mean it, Alan. Either you explain this game to me or I'm going to be asking lots of silly questions and you'll get *very* annoyed. Really, it's for your own good.'

'Why now? There's been cricket since, oh, since 1066.'

'Why now? Because now I want to learn. I think.'

'Since before we married.'

'We're still married.'

'Okay.' He makes a familiar gesture: he locks his hands and pushes them out in front of him with the palms outwards and his fingers tensed. His wedding ring is partly obscured.

'This goes on for five days, doesn't it?'

'I said okay.' The highlights have resumed. 'Over supper.'

For a brief moment the camera turns to the scoreboard, a cluster of numbers like Sudoku but one stands out: 'Last man: 8.' On what scale? If 1 to 10 then he must have been good; was it just that someone better came along?

I slide down on the sofa. During the second break I look round and see that Agnieszka has joined us, watching from the doorway. I can feel her bewilderment gathering, like an itch at the back of my neck, and eventually it breaks. 'What is happening?' she asks, echoing my own question of only a few minutes before, but Alan takes her question as referring specifically to the fact the game has been interrupted while the umpires and the batters stop for a chat in the middle of the field.

'The batsmen are being offered the light,' Alan says.

'Which light?' Agnieszka asks.

'Well, that's the point,' Alan says. 'There isn't much light at all, it's getting dark, and if the umpires think the batsmen can't see the ball very well they give them the option of stopping now and calling it a day.'

The players are going off the field. The umpires are picking up the wooden sticks.

'So now we can eat?' Agnieszka says, and I know what's going to come next: the salt and pepper grinders as the umpires or the batters or the wooden sticks, our glasses being moved around, Alan speaking slowly in words of one syllable, Agnieszka asking him to repeat these words and how to spell them. But there will be learning and enlightenment without me having to talk at all, I will simply absorb.

So it happens.

Each team has eleven players. One team sends in its first two people to bat and the other team tries to get them out. This is simple, after all, and because Agnieszka is looking serious and not flustered I know that she too is enlarging her understanding of the world. The ways in which the batters can be got out are manifold: bowled, caught, leg before wicket, stumped, run out. From a slight hesitation in Alan's voice I can tell that these are not the only ways, but he doesn't want to confuse us, not yet. The batters' job is to hit the ball and run between the sticks of wood before the other side can get it back, or hit the ball out of the field. They score runs. When one batter is out another one comes in, until they've all had a turn. Then the other team bats.

Agnieszka asks if the referee has a whistle, like in football.

Alan explains about the umpires.

'What happens if the ball hits one of these men?'

He draws in his breath.

'And on TV,' Agnieszka continues, 'I saw a bird on the field, I think a seagull. What happens if the ball hits the seagull?'

Alan says the bird would fly away before it was hit.

'But is the ball a hard ball? If it hits the seagull, would the seagull get killed?'

Alan thinks it would.

Agnieszka shivers. I say the food is good, which it is, chicken and tomatoes and some kind of beans, which we are eating with bread, but Alan says it was meant to be hotter than this, next time he will put in more spices than the recipe says.

'Can girls play cricket?' Agnieszka asks.

'They can,' says Alan. But for some reason not many of them choose to.

'When girls play cricket, do the referees must also be girls?'

Alan pours more wine into his glass and looks at the ceiling.

'Really,' says Agnieszka, 'I know this is trouble, but if no one asks questions then all is ignorance and darkness.'

I touch her arm, but immediately she stands up and starts to clear the table. I notice that she has pushed all her chicken to the side of her plate and half-hidden it under a slice of bread: she is apparently going through one of her vegetarian phases, which come and go, and which Alan—and I too, sometimes—tends to be slow on picking up on, because she doesn't like making an issue of it. I follow her into the kitchen, spoon the remaining food from the serving dish onto a plate for Selwyn and look round for somewhere to place it. Agnieszka takes the plate from me and puts it into the oven. She tells me to go and rest.

I DON'T WANT to rest. This mood I was in when I came into the house, when I told Alan his apron needed washing, is back on me. I go upstairs to Selwyn's room and knock on the door. I go in and sit on his bed. Clothes everywhere, the smell of socks, the little green standby lights on his TV and laptop still on. There's broken glass on the carpet beside his desk. I was sixteen too, once upon a time. I start to look for his mobile phone. Selwyn is often out but usually phones to say when he's coming back and if he wants supper keeping, or if he's staying over at a friend's.

Really, I am happy, I am loved.

Agnieszka shouts from downstairs that she is going out, and the door slams behind her.

No footsteps, no traffic even. The house is completely silent. I begin to make Selwyn's bed, first shifting the duvet so I can pull the sheet to the sides, and there is the black controller thing that he uses for his computer games, like a dead beetle on the pillow. Now tidying his room seems completely the wrong thing to do, so I stop, leaving the duvet in a heap, and go down to the kitchen.

Alan is sitting at the table, making a map of the solar system. I guess that he's been talking with Agnieszka, while doing the washing up, about astronomy, or some new planet they've discovered. I sit down opposite him, watching his pencil move across the paper, until I notice that the names he is writing in are not those of the planets.

'Alan—'

'Look, these are the fielding positions. I think I've got most of them. Do you want to see?'

First slip. Second slip, third slip—there are a lot. In fact there seem to be far more than eleven. Square leg. Gully. Midwicket. Point. Long off, long on.

'These are for a right-handed batsman, of course. But for a left-handed one they just switch over.'

I notice that when he talks to me in this very determined, very rational way, it's like he's the one who's been cheating and he's making it all up as he goes along. '*We had to finish the presentation for Monday. For the shoe people, you know? I'm sure I told you. And we couldn't get the figures until Tokyo closed.*'

We look at each other encouragingly.

'Like when you're looking in the mirror,' he says.

'Oh?'

'When they switch over, I mean. For a batsman who's left-handed. Like when you look in the mirror and your right becomes your left—'

'Does it?'

I look towards the patio doors, where my reflection

appears in the dark glass as if I'm outside, looking in from the garden. I raise my left foot.

'I was making it for Agnieszka,' Alan continues. 'She seems really keen.'

'It's lovely, Alan. I'm sure she'll—'

'But if you—'

'No, I couldn't. This is Agnieszka's—'

'Go on, take it.' He pushes this map across the table towards me. 'I can easily do another.'

Fine leg. Third man. Silly mid-on.

His right hand moves towards me and then circles the outside of the map. 'When they're further out, they're generally called *deep*. And further in, *short*.'

'Yes.'

'These are just the *possible* positions, of course. They're not all used at the same time. It depends who's batting, and how the bowler is bowling. So that's why there's so many of them.'

'I was wondering about that.'

'It's yours. Please.'

He gets up to find another piece of paper, for a second solar system. A parallel universe. For a moment I think of asking him to mark North, then I fold my map into four and hold it.

'Are you busy tomorrow, by the way?' he asks.

'If there's anything—'

'No, nothing we need. And we're going out tomorrow night, remember? Jamal and what's-her-name. It's just that I've got these tickets for the cricket for tomorrow, for Selwyn and me, and if Selwyn's not around then I thought, Agnieszka?'

'Perfect.'

'But if you'd rather—'

'No. I've already got her map.'

He looks at me, checking.

'I mean it, Alan. You go with Agnieszka. It'll be really special for her.'

I take the pencil from his hand and walk over to the worktop to sharpen it with a kitchen knife.

LATER, IN THE bathroom. Selwyn's toothbrush is still here. And there, higher up, lying on top of the cupboard for medicines and spare razor blades and six-year-old half-used bottles of tea-tree shampoo for hair lice, is his mobile phone.

What happens if the ball hits the seagull?

No wonder Agnieszka's questions annoy Alan: they are ones that need asking. If no one gets a batter out, does he go on batting for five days? If the umpire makes a decision that is obviously wrong, does everyone still have to obey him? If everyone agrees, can you change the rules? What happens if the loss-adjuster has a terrible car accident and loses both legs, or if I forget his telephone number?

A boy goes missing and who can blame him? He doesn't *mean* to go missing.

He is sixteen years old and his clothes are falling off him and his father is at work in an office that he used to think was important and his step-mother is with her lover and downstairs is a girl who used to be the au pair and is somehow still here, after so many years, as a constant reminder that his bottom used to need wiping. He is sitting in his room and he is watching TV: someone hits someone else and the second person hits the first person back. He's so bored that he feels he's been sitting in this room his whole life, staring at men hitting each other and old posters of Bart Simpson dating from the time it was exciting to say words like 'bum,' and waiting for other people to stop talking and pay him some attention, and everything else has been a dream. Or else this is the dream and he is in it, and something has to break—*loudly*, and into lots of pieces—for him to wake up. So he starts throwing balled-up socks at the beer glass on his desk that holds his old pens and he hears his step-mother's voice: 'What if everyone started throwing socks at beer glasses?' This is familiar: what if *everyone* picked their noses in public or shouted out swear words or put their hand inside their trousers and scratched? But they wouldn't. Or at least, not all at the same time.

Then his step-mother apologizes for speaking to him the way she did and this is sad, almost as sad as the way his parents spend years of their lives fussing about his table manners or whether he's cleaned his teeth or his toenails need cutting or he's getting enough vitamin A or B or Q and then suddenly they stop, they ignore him completely, as if the whole family thing has just been a game to pass the time, like throwing balled-up socks. Although after they've dropped out of the game they still insist, when they bother to notice that he's still around, that the rules apply to *him*, and that his vitamin levels are the most important things in his life.

So the boy walks out of his house and catches a bus into town and when he gets off he sees a small crowd of people gathered on the pavement up a side street. They are watching something happen and they are very quiet and then they are all talking and excited and then they go quiet again. The boy walks towards these people and because they are coming and going and moving around, and because they are slower than him and there are spaces that he can move into but they can't, pretty soon he's near the front.

A man wearing a flat leather cap is doing the three-card trick on an upturned box. A punter puts money on the box and the man shows him three cards and then places them face down and shuffles them, fast, and the punter points to the one he thinks is the queen of spades and he's wrong, and the man pockets his fiver. But there's a man wearing glasses in the crowd who sometimes gets it right—which encourages others to lay down their money and lose it.

The boy puts a five-pound note on the box. The man looks at him and smiles but his eyes don't. The man shows the cards and the boy nods and then holds his breath, shutting out everything around him, as the man moves the cards around in a flurry. When the man stops the boy points to the queen of spades.

He's right, he knows he is. But the card man cheats. He picks up, not the card the boy is pointing to, but the one next to it, and he shows the two of diamonds and shakes his head and the boy's fiver has already disappeared. And before the boy can say or do anything about this other things are happening around him. '*Police!*' The crowd is dispersing and the man has kicked over the box and is quickly walking away, his hands jammed down hard in his pockets, with the other man wearing glasses beside him.

The boy follows them. They turn left, and when the boy reaches the corner he sees that they are running.

At the next junction two men separate. They are both wearing black jackets, dark trousers. The boy follows the card man—he thinks it's the card man, but he isn't nearly so sure as he was about the queen of spades. He runs down a street of shops that are closed and then a street of much taller buildings with balconies overhead and washing hanging out and then he turns another corner and for a moment he thinks the man has escaped, the street is empty and silent and all he can hear is the pounding of his own heart. But his eyes catch a sudden movement next to a lamp-post about twenty yards away and there the man is, glancing back.

The boy starts running again. A dog springs out of a doorway and snaps at his heels but he ignores it. This movement, he begins to understand, is good, much better than throwing balled-up socks. He could go on for ever. It doesn't matter now whether he's chasing anyone or not, and the money doesn't matter either.

The boy follows the man across a street, not bothering to look out for traffic. Then one more corner, a short road between closed garages and warehouses, and suddenly the boy is out in the open, at the edge of a wide road with busy traffic, two lanes on each side and low metal barriers on a strip of dirty grass in the middle. The man runs across the first two lanes, just in front of a row of cars that are picking up speed after being stopped at a red light, and skips over the barrier. By the time the boy crosses the cars are travelling fast, a horn sounds loudly and far too close and a car brakes and swerves.

At the barrier the boy stops. His head is buzzing, his whole body trembling. The man has disappeared. He could have gone either left or right. He could have doubled back at the traffic lights. More likely he's somewhere in the rough ground on the other side of the road with tough, spiky bushes and a row of parked trucks against a wall. By now it's too dark to see. The boy has been running for hours.

He grips the metal barrier as trucks thunder past, just inches away, blowing waves of dust and hot exhaust fumes in his face. He feels that he's been shuffled and lost, and has been lost for some time now, much longer than tonight. He thinks it's probably a natural condition, which the rules of the family game are there to disguise, and now he'll have to get used to it. But if it involves running, it will be okay. He has expended a huge amount of energy and has passed over into somewhere new. He has the feeling that he's just run a race, and because there's no one in front of him he must have won. He deserves a prize, a medal with a ribbon at the very least, even if he doesn't have a bedroom wall to hang it on.

THIS IS THE story I tell my lover. I'm lying down, again, which is why it goes on a bit. This is the story I tell the loss-adjuster, for that is his job, and I hope to God he's good at it.

'Where did the three-card man come from?' he asks.

'I passed one on the way here. Round the corner from the Tube station.'

'He's a gypsy, I suppose?'

'I imagine so.'

'You imagine. Could be a lot worse.'

'I don't want to go there.'

'Don't.'

'He's stayed out one night. He's done this before, he was staying over at a friend's, he's probably fine. I can still choose.'

'Good choice.'

'Mmm?'

'Yes?'

'What's the score?'

'You really want to know?'

'I couldn't give a fuck.'

'180 for 2. India were all out for 198. Have you done anything? Called the police?'

'Alan called them this morning. I made him.'

'Because you think if it comes from a man, they take it more—'

'But they do, don't they?'

I LIE WITH this loss-adjuster not making love. It's a thing that lovers are for.

And then we do, because it's another thing they're for, and I want to. I can still choose.

Afterwards, which is in fact a lot later, I sit with my knees up looking out of the window. The loss-adjuster, I think, has an inkling to turn on the TV, but I'm not going to tell him he can. I'm busy.

'What are you doing?' he asks.

'I'm training my eyes.'

'How do you train your eyes?'

'By counting the bricks in that wall.'

'How many?'

'I get up to nineteen and then I lose track, so I start

again. But the next time I only get up to twelve, and the time after that it's down to three. It's not going well.'

If I turn to him he will see that I'm crying. When I turn to him. When he makes me turn to him.

IT'S RAINING. THE players are off the field. They don't want to get their white trousers muddy. Alan will have seen the forecast, will have taken an umbrella, will be holding it over Agnieszka who actually *likes* the rain and would prefer to be getting wet. If you turn on the TV, the game you are seeing is not the game you at first think you are seeing but the recorded highlights of another, previous, historic game. You can probably tell, if you know about these things, how long ago this game was by tiny differences in fashion: the boots, the bagginess of the clothes, the peaks of their caps.

So: how the loss-adjuster and I met.

I was at a translators' conference in Edinburgh. (I have two jobs, both of them small, one of which is translating from the Spanish. My father was Spanish. But that can keep till another rainy day.) He too was at a conference, for loss-adjusters, at the same hotel, and because his conference was even more tedious than mine he decided to pay mine a visit. He arrived in the middle of a session and sat in the row behind me; and though I didn't turn round the notes I was taking became illegible, and then stopped altogether. On the transparently ridiculous grounds that he wanted to learn more about translation as a form of neo-colonialism, he suggested we have dinner. Which, given how little we ate, went on for a very long time. Loss-adjusters earn more than translators, and he had a room at the hotel. I phoned the people I was staying with, friends of Alan who lived in Edinburgh, and told them not to wait up.

We walked and talked and lay down. Except for the weather and the traffic and the tall grey buildings, it was bucolic: we were shepherds somewhere remote, or shepherd and shepherdess. I had a dictionary, he a calculator. Poems are what get lost in translation, he translated losses into finite figures. One bright and blustery afternoon we were sitting out at a café by the docks in Leith and I wanted to show him a story I was translating. As I took the folder from my bag the pages fell out and were blown up among the gulls and out over the edge of the quay. The loss-adjuster jumped up and began to chase after them, stumbling and grabbing at what the wind tore away. He looked as though he was being attacked by a swarm of bees or his house was burning down and he was trying to save the one thing important to him, except that the thing was mine and it wasn't important at all, and besides I had saved the file.

On the Friday evening Alan came up from London

to spend the weekend with me. We went out for a meal: Alan, me, Alan's friends, and the loss-adjuster came too and kept ordering more wine. He got into a fight with two men at the next table who he said were laughing at me, or staring, or anyway something that he decided was offensive. Almost certainly something very small, like the color of their ties. He stood up and told them to apologize. He was gripping a chair, hard, in order to stand up, and I remember praying he wouldn't let go. When one of the men told him to sit down and stop making an idiot of himself, the loss-adjuster hit him. The woman at our table, the wife of Alan's friend, had a giggling fit.

A month later he wrote to me. His handwriting— oddly old-fashioned and impersonal—was that of someone who'd been taught at school how to hold a pen properly. He wrote that he was surprised by how easy it had been to hit someone, to throw a punch; his hand didn't hurt at all, though doubtless it would have been different if he'd been sober. He wrote that he was going on a business trip to Spain, and as he didn't know any Spanish and the phrase books he had looked at weren't helpful, perhaps I could provide him with translations for some essential sentences. *I am lost. Do I have to change trains? Please give me directions to your bedroom.*

HE DOES HAVE a name—it might even have been pinned to his jacket at the conference hotel—but I don't want to use it in case it breaks.

I MUST HAVE dozed. The dream that's with me in mid-flow when I wake up has something to do with the story whose pages blew away on Leith docks, except that the loss-adjuster is in it and the sentence I'm knitting my brow over, trying to fit the words to the rhythm and balance, is an exquisitely formal little piece of work. It reminds me of being on the top floor of the V&A, looking at those polished brass instruments for finding where you are in the middle of the ocean. They have tiny coiled springs and cogs that slot together so perfectly you could become hypnotized watching them and scales marked in minuscule units of measurement, but they are trained on the stars, or the horizon. '*If the loss-adjuster had not been so continuously something, I would surely have something to something something.*'

The eighteenth century: I think I am a bluestocking. My father would have been proud. (The loss-adjuster unrolling my blue stockings, his fingers light on the mesh . . .)

What has woken me is the sound of the loss-adjuster chuckling. 'Look at this,' he says.

On the TV, men in bright yellow jackets are running across the cricket field. A bomb? An injury?—but the loss-adjuster finds it funny. Then the camera shows why: ahead of the men in yellow, almost in the middle of the field, is a naked man. Now he's on the center strip, the area of almost brown earth, and he's jumping in the air, his penis bobbling. The camera immediately cuts away to the dark-skinned umpire, who is looking down at his watch.

I stare hungrily, impatiently, because it was only a moment, two seconds of fame at most, that the camera granted the naked man, but it was enough. This isn't a man at all. It's Selwyn.

I swallow hard. Relief—that he's there, and visible. I get up from the bed and start dressing, hurriedly. The TV shows a gang of at least six yellow-jacketed men dragging Selwyn off the field.

'Where are you going?' asks the loss-adjuster.

'Where,' I ask him, 'do they take him now, that man?'

The loss-adjuster looks at me as if I've started speaking in Spanish. Which I do, sometimes, on occasions of high emotion, but not this time. I'm staying grounded, practical.

When he realizes I'm waiting for an answer, he says

he doesn't know. 'The Tower of London. The local police station.'

'Do they go back and collect his clothes before they set off? Or does he have to go in the van naked?'

'They'll give him a blanket, I guess.'

'A *blanket*? Do police vans carry blankets, and duvets and pillow cases? Do they handcuff him?'

'Why are you asking?'

'Because that's Selwyn!' I'm angry not with him, but because I can't find a shoe.

'Oh,' he says. 'Oh. I don't think so.'

'You've never seen him.' Not even a photograph. How *can* I have not shown him?

'No, but it's unlikely.'

'When did unlikely stop something being true?'

'When you're tired. And worried.'

'Wrong answer.'

'That's a common-or-garden streaker. They come from nowhere, they parade their dicks or their breasts to a national audience, they go on a couple of chat shows, they disappear. It's a tradition.'

I sit down on the bed, still one-shoed. At least, I think, Selwyn is safe, and in a particular place. They're probably taking his fingerprints right now: those unique whorls, no one else's in the universe. 'You're telling me,'

I say calmly—but clearly I *am* angry with him, the shoe is secondary—'that a mother doesn't know her own son?'

'You are not his mother.'

'I have seen that boy naked more times than any other person on this planet.'

'Step-mother.'

This hurts. 'No. No and no and no. You think because I'm his step-mother I can't know him better than his what, his *biological* mother? Love him better? Biology has nothing to do with this, it's not even on the syllabus. If you think I'm deliberately trying to love him more precisely because I didn't see him hauled out in a bloody bundle from between my legs—if you think I'm like those women in the City who whine that they have to work harder than the men just to stay equal, to prove themselves—or like some bloody cricketer with a limp who's trying to disguise it so he can play with the others—if you think this is what I've been doing with my life then truly, you don't understand the world. I love that boy. Full stop. And I don't know what I'm doing here.'

I'm not going to lie down and look under the bed while he's standing up. I set off towards the door, carrying my one shoe in my hand.

He puts a hand on my shoulder, then on my cheek.

He kisses me. He tells me to wait. He tells me he'll find out where Selwyn is.

I sit down again on the bed while he phones. On the TV the cricket has resumed. Who is he phoning? He gets stuck in a queuing system, a menu, a *following list of options*. Press 1 for murder, 2 to report a stolen chicken. I go for a pee and find my shoe behind the bathroom door and have a sudden flashback of how it got there. I can hear his teeth grit, I can hear him saying, 'No, I don't want to report a crime, but I will happily commit one if it will make you listen to me.'

I put on my shoes, he puts on his. We leave the flat, get in the car, start driving towards the cricket ground to find the nearest police station. The traffic is no better than always. I think that by the time we get there the evening paper will be out on the news-stands, or tomorrow morning's, with a photo of Selwyn naked on the front page.

There is an insect in the car, and then I realize it's the loss-adjuster humming. Alan too does this, tunes from old musicals. He's actually enjoying himself, having something to do, a man thing.

We find a police station, any building at all as long as it has policemen inside it. The scratched desk, glum eyes, the interruptions. Slumped on a hard bench, watching us, is a woman in a dressing gown who looks as if she's lost not just a son but everything she ever had. It takes a hundred years, even after we've used the word 'mother,' which jumps us forward six squares, up a ladder. Mandatory orientation courses and consultation exercises have trained these men to recognize this word: it means trouble, it means deal with and get rid of as soon as possible. Phone calls, computer crashes, abort/retry/cancel, more phone calls. It turns out that the name of the streaker on the cricket ground this afternoon is Simon. Close, but not an exact match. Age thirty-four, occupation trainee accountant, place of residence Balham. Simon someone. Someone else.

EXTRAS: THE SMALL mistakes you make, the runs that you gift to the other team, without them having to do anything to gain them. A lack of discipline. They don't usually amount to much, not enough to affect the result.

ON THE WAY back from the police station the loss-adjuster drops me at the Tube station. The gypsy is there, the one who does the three-card tick, round the corner from the entrance. He's short, black-haired, and has oddly large hands. He nods at me as if in recognition.

Surprised, I look away, pretending I haven't been staring at him.

And then I'm staring at someone else: on the pavement outside a kebab shop I see a boy—youth, man— wearing Selwyn's tee-shirt, the one with the words that would make me want to hit him if I was gay, the one we talked about but which he carries on wearing. I look back to the card-man, who shakes his head.

Alan and Agnieszka are at home. But we are not going out to Jamal and what's-her-name's for dinner tonight. Jamal phoned Alan this morning to say he was in the middle, or perhaps only at the beginning, of a row with his girlfriend and couldn't see that dinner tonight would be possible, unless we wanted to come and cook it ourselves while the cutlery flew through the air around us. Then the girlfriend phoned to say come. Then Jamal phoned again to say don't come.

'We should go,' I say.

'But Jamal—'

'Long day's journey into night. It'll be fun.'

'But Jamal—'

'Alan, they're obviously on a day-trip to hell and at least we'd provide some distraction. Slow down the descent.'

Agnieszka looks at her watch, a black and clunky new one. 'So they can come up for air, a bit?' she says.

'But Jamal doesn't *want* us to come,' says Alan. 'And he's the one we know, it's him I'm listening to.'

'He's embarrassed,' I say. 'He wanted to show off his new teenage girlfriend and now it's all gone wrong and her make-up's all streaky and her hair's in a mess and he doesn't want us to see her.'

'Right. So we don't go.'

'Ask him to come here. He's probably just realized that his girlfriend is turning into his wife and he's desperate to get out. He's your friend, call him. It's what men do for each other, isn't it?'

'But he can't come here because of the cat. He gets his asthma, he can't breathe, you know that.'

We glare at each other. Whatever I say next, he will have an answer to. He has, the commentator would say, worked me out.

Then Alan's mobile rings. Jamal.

'Oh, good,' Alan says on the phone. 'Fine . . . No, really, that's fine. And you know, thank you for calling, I mean it . . . Well, we *were* a bit worried, but—. . . So you're okay? You don't need—. . . Yes, good . . . Yes, of course I will . . . Bye.'

He puts his phone down on the table.

44

'So?'

'That was Selwyn,' he says. 'He's with Rashid.'

I stare, dumbfounded. Knocked not sideways but inwards, so I have to wait before I can speak until my body has regained its functioning shape. Why didn't he pass the phone to me? Why can't *I* speak to my son?

Agnieszka vanishes. I think she's said something about going to get a takeaway.

Then worse. I can't call Selwyn because his phone's upstairs. He was phoning from his friend's mobile, the friend he's staying with. But the number must now be on Alan's mobile? We retrieve it. I call. The phone has been switched off.

He's all right, Alan assures me. Selwyn is sixteen and staying with a friend we know and has phoned home—we should be grateful, not worried. And Alan is clearly more interested in talking about the cricket than about Selwyn. England were 243 for 4 at the close, pretty slow progress, but they lost a lot of time because of interruptions. They had to stop early because the light was bad, and it rained for some time in the early afternoon, and then there was a streaker, this naked man running across the pitch. Agnieszka, apparently, thoroughly enjoyed it. She thought the streaker was all part of the game, a ploy by the bowling side to distract the batsmen and stop them getting runs.

'Actually,' I tell Alan, 'right now I don't want to hear about the cricket.'

Agnieszka arrives with takeaway Indian food: rice, chapatis, chickpeas, something muddy and greenish for herself and two charred, cold and vividly red chicken breasts for Alan and me.

While we are eating Agnieszka tells us that she has lost her shiny gold pen, which is not as important as losing a son but it matters to her. On the other hand, she has obviously gained this black and complicated object on her wrist. I can guess from looking at it where it comes from, but I think she would like to tell me herself so I ask if it's the kind of watch that can tell you what time it is in different places.

'Why do I want to know so many times?' she replies. 'One is enough. This watch is for diving in the sea.'

I nod. This will be more fun than crosswords, surely.

'It tells you how deep you are and makes alarm if no more air. Also the time, of course.' She holds it to her ear, as if to check whether the alarm is sounding and she's running out of oxygen. 'From Harvey,' she adds.

'Tell me, Agnieszka, does Harvey teach a course in

deep-sea diving?' It seems unlikely, but he doesn't look like my idea of a teacher of childcare either. Agnieszka wants to be a paediatric nurse.

'No, Harvey is not a teacher.'

'But you met him at the college?'

'He comes there every day now.'

'So he's a student?'

'No, not a student. He sits in the bar, but it's not a real bar.'

'You mean, this college isn't really a college at all?' says Alan, confused.

'It doesn't sell beer, just coffee and drinks from a machine. The coffee is horrible but cheap, very cheap.' Agnieszka has always been economical. She makes egg sandwiches to take to college. Her mother has a good job and she doesn't send money home so perhaps she is saving, I think, to get married. This is something both admirable and deeply sad, and it makes me shiver. It reminds me of when, a year ago, I looked in Selwyn's math homework book—pages and pages of neatly ranged sums, some of the figures crossed out and redone, which after the exam would be thrown away, and probably the knowledge too, forgotten, never to be used again—and I cried.

'And Harvey sits in this bar all day?'

'He does crosswords.'

'Of course.'

Alan tries a forkful of Agnieszka's greenish curry. He seems worried, and only in part because he can't identify what vegetables he's eating. 'Doesn't he have anything else to do, Agnieszka? Doesn't he have a job?'

'He's very good at crosswords. He goes to some other places too, like art galleries and hotels. And the park in summertime.'

Ah. He picks up girls. He offers private lessons.

'Two weeks ago,' Agnieszka adds, 'he went to Heathrow.'

'To wait for someone?'

'No.'

This isn't enough for Alan. 'Agnieszka,' he says, 'we're very glad you're going to the college. Because it will help you get a job, a good job.'

'I hope so.'

'And a job's important, don't you think? Everyone needs a job. This vegetable thing, by the way, is very good.'

'But Harvey—'

'Crosswords are a hobby, Agnieszka. They're not a job, not real work. They're what you do when you come home from work, to relax. They're like stamp-collecting, or golf, or hang-gliding.'

Hang-gliding? Has he mentioned this before?

'Without work,' Alan continues, 'proper work, you're wasting your life a bit, don't you think? And someone who doesn't have a job—well, I mean, it's something you need to do, to establish yourself, it's all to do with who you are . . . '

He's struggling here. He looks to me for support.

MY OTHER SMALL job is teaching the history of science in an art college. Like teaching atheism in a seminary, or pot-holing to airline pilots, and at first that was the point of it: fun, and perversity, besides all the stuff I filled in on the forms like introducing the students to alternative ways of making sense of the world, blah. But now the job is small not just because art-college terms are short but because I, or the students, or all of us, have lost interest. It's an option or module or something, and because it's a module that very few of the students now bother to choose I have only two regulars: a mature student called Richard, an ex-policeman, who has no artistic talent at all and why he's at the college anyway I don't know, and Helga, who is eighteen and speaks hardly any

English and is in love with me. There's nothing I can do about this.

All of the students know far more about science and technology than I do. They cut films, operate sound systems, create special effects, find ways of talking for hours on the phone with their gap-year lovers in Australia and Argentina without having to pay a penny. I can cut and paste in Word, change a light bulb and adjust the timer on the central heating. But I do have a lingering and admittedly barely professional interest in the history of technology, or more specifically, how things came into being. If I'm passing a second-hand book stall, I still stop if I see something big and brightly colored and called *A Hundred Great Inventions*.

The wheel, for example. It serves a purpose and is a completely obvious and necessary thing to have. Why the Incas, who built roads aplenty, somehow missed out on inventing the wheel remains a mystery to me, though I do know it's a mystery that somehow concerns the llama. And roast pork, which according to Charles Lamb, who himself had the tale from Confucius, was invented in China by Bobo. This boy, bored witless at home while his father was out herding swine, started playing with matches and managed to set the whole house on fire with nine pigs still inside it, and the smell of roasting meat had the neighbors salivating.

Not matches, exactly. Rubbing two sticks together was more Bobo's thing; matches didn't arrive until the middle of the nineteenth century. By which time cricket had been up and running for two hundred years, longer, and you have to ask: why?

What's it for? What does it do or provide that couldn't be done or provided by some other and much simpler means? Without cricket, would the history of the world have been different?

There's both a serenity and a dizziness to these questions, and I like the mix. A lighter, more abstract version of what happens when I think about the loss-adjuster. At the micro level too: how different would English summers be without slip fielders? If there were five or nine balls in an over and not six? If the loss-adjuster was right-handed and not left-handed?

'I'M GOING TO look for Agnieszka's pen,' I say, pushing all my unfinished food in Alan's direction. 'I think I've seen it somewhere upstairs.'

I have no idea where the thing is. Besides, this is Selwyn's job, not mine: looking for lost pens, and finding them. I just want to get away. Not that anyone will notice my disappearance: I am not needed, superfluous. Selwyn doesn't want to talk to me, Alan decides our social life, Agnieszka's moral welfare has been taken out of my hands.

I knock on Selwyn's door and go in: absence, and the duvet massed into a heap where I left it only makes the absence more obvious. I wander into our room and sit on the bed for several minutes fiddling with the alarm clock before I realize where I need to be: somewhere small and cramped and black.

There is a cupboard under the stairs: you can't stand up, the light bulb doesn't work, hanging from nails are musty old coats and a pair of binoculars and the chain-and-leather lead of a much-loved dog that died in agony under the wheels of a removal van. It is a dungeon, a place of bondage and punishment, and it's where Agnieszka finds me. I have tripped over a heap of rubber boots and have fallen awkwardly on something hard and sharp and screamed to high heaven.

The door opens, light floods in.

Agnieszka hauls me upright. She is very strong—an essential qualification, when we took her into this house. She could pick up Selwyn with one hand, she could drag a mattress out to the garden to air after a bed-wetting incident with no more effort than if she was carrying a bag of peanuts. I imagine that she comes from a family of farmers or lumberjacks, not office workers. Her eyes are shining—she is excited to be helping, this is some kind of emergency fieldwork for her childcare course. But then I see she is not looking at me at all. She is looking beyond me, at something in the cupboard. And now she is pushing past me, shoving the coats aside and dragging out her prey from behind a defunct upright hoover—a cricket set, bat and wooden sticks in a plastic bag, smaller than I'd remembered but then so many things and places in one's past, when revisited, appear to have shrunk.

'Oh,' I say, closing my eyes to deal with the shock of memories surging in, a time when Selwyn was just eight or nine years old.

To begin with all was good will and enthusiasm. Alan said that Selwyn had a natural talent. I laughed. A natural talent for swimming, I could understand. Or running. Or drinking wine or telling jokes or sex. All these are normal, rational human activities, and I can see why God might enjoy scattering at random a few especially gifted individuals—to set some standards, to give the rest of us something to live up to. The government would call them beacons of excellence. But for cricket—which may well be the most over-designed of all human activities, and is neither normal nor rational—surely no one can have a *natural* talent.

Alan did persevere. He got together a group of maybe half a dozen boys of Selwyn's age in the park on Sunday mornings. I watched from an outdoor table at the café as he demonstrated the cover drive, flailing his bat towards a scampering squirrel. I watched him hold the ball in his hand and give it a sudden twist, as if he was shutting off the water mains. That café served a very good home-made lemon cake. But over the summer the group fell away. By late July only Alan, Selwyn and Rashid remained, and to Rashid's bowling Alan had no answer, which was all the more humiliating given how slowly and languidly Rashid sent the ball towards him. The cricket set found its home at the back of the cupboard under the stairs, as I have too.

Back in the kitchen, Agnieszka and Alan chatter merrily over their new prize. Alan takes out the bat and poses in the batter's correct stance; because the bat is for an eight-year-old he's bending over more than seems comfortable, as if he's stooping to look for a coin that's rolled underneath the cooker. Agnieszka examines the stumps and the tiny bits that go on top as if she's just unpacked a flat-pack shelving kit and there are pieces missing, or too many pieces. Again I am superfluous.

But apparently not.

As I start to clear the takeaway cartons from the table Agnieszka looks up at me and then runs from the room. Seconds later she reappears in the kitchen doorway, holding her hands behind her back. She beams; and whatever is coming next, I know she means well. Suddenly one hand thrusts forward and offers me a black Waterstones bag. 'For you.'

Inside is an enormous yellow book: *Wisden's Cricketers' Almanac.*

'Oh, Agnieszka, thank you,' I say. '*Wisden.*'

'Wisdom.'

'Of a kind, I suppose.'

'No, it's the best. There is nothing other to compare with this. For longer than a hundred years. Really, this is the Bible.'

The book is so heavy I have sat down. It weighs in my lap. I check the last page number: 1,664.

'Read this tonight, please,' Agnieszka says. 'And tomorrow, at two o'clock you must be here. Not late.'

Friday | Saturday | **Sunday** | Monday | Tuesday

'What are you thinking about?'

'Love.'

'In general, or in particular?'

'In particular. You?'

'Ants. Oh, and hanging, shooting, drowning or poison.'

'Are you asking me to choose?'

NOTHING HAPPENS, MUCH. Then something does. Then nothing again, or—rarely—something else. Then nothing, and so on and so on until it becomes hard to perceive any difference between nothing and something.

To break the rhythm, to introduce a little visual diversity, the camera sometimes cuts to close-up shots of the spectators, magaziney girls with big breasts or men dressed as carrots. Today, it has twice homed in on a man in a wheelchair wearing black glasses. He is staring at the players with absolute concentration, and even before the camera moved back a smidgeon so you could see his white stick and his guide dog, I knew he was blind.

For perhaps 95 per cent of the time, for those who have no strong interest in what they are looking at, it is dull. Even Alan can't convince me that watching the bowler walk back to the place where he starts his run-up makes for edge-of-your-seat viewing, or the times after each over when they all move to different positions and start again from the other end. The effect, I suppose, is to make the fun bits—like when the batter really smashes the ball, or someone leaps in the air and falls flat—more exciting, worth waiting for. Yesterday someone complained about the ball so they brought out a box of other ones and the umpire offered the box to the players to choose from. The strawberry cream? The walnut truffle? No one ever chooses the nougat, I don't know why they bother.

I think of Alan and me sitting at the kitchen table having one of our fumbling arguments, with Selwyn as spectator. It doesn't matter what it's about: do we go by Tube or take the car, do we really need a new computer and why not second-hand, how much can you still like someone if they believe in God or send their children to private schools. When one of us is on top form, it might be diverting. When both of us are, it's entertaining, for us too. If it's a flat pitch and the ball isn't turning and we're just going through the motions, he walks out. 'Selwyn, come back!' Alan pleads. 'Why don't we . . . '

Alan doesn't approve of boredom. It makes him feel guilty. This is because he's not good at it. So he devotes enormous amounts of energy to doing battle with it: making lists and plans, being better at his job than his colleagues, cleaning his shoes, getting up early on holiday so we can fit in the flea-market and the ice-cream place before the transport museum. And, yes, watching cricket. Because I'm better at being bored, the fact that I find pretty well all of the above boring (although I did unexpectedly enjoy the transport museum) hasn't mattered, much. He used to worry about Selwyn not being 'stimulated' enough, but a lot of the time that was because he was jealous of Selwyn for being even better at boredom than me, or for not seeing it as a problem, or for not being bored at all.

Ants—an obvious, indeed hackneyed example. I'm sure Selwyn isn't the only child who has spent an enraptured two hours watching ants drag a couple of bread-crumbs or a scrap of apple peel across the draining board, along the wall, up between the window frame and where the draught excluder's come loose, down again, through the jagged peaks and vast crevasses of the patio and down into a black hole. The leaders, the laggards, those who are doomed. Diversions, heavier loads, new obstacles put in place. Calculated floods. While I watched him from where I was sitting, as he watched the ants, and Alan fretted that if we didn't set off *now* for wherever we'd intended to go there'd be nothing to see when we got there. Wordsworthian, this: the natural world, all those vivid sense impressions. Not that nature need have anything to do with it. Screwdrivers were magic. A wet afternoon would enable Selwyn to discover exactly how many different parts the hoover was made up of, and the wonderful properties of accumulated dust: how it adheres, how it hangs in the air and disperses. Or the tripod for Alan's camera, or his desk lamp, which by the extreme mercy of a usually non-existent beneficent god was un-plugged at the time. ('The un-making of things can have as creative results as the making of them: discuss'—a question I'd include in my History of Science exam, if they ever went back to setting exams.) Nor, I believe, when Selwyn was walking home with Rashid from pri-mary school, same route every day for years, were they bored or silent: they debated passionately whether it would be better to die from too much heat or too much cold, and the gloriously many different ways of committing suicide.

But it's different now. He sits in front of a computer game on a flat screen—and this *is* boring, because he knows how these games will end, or at any rate the people who make them do: they're finite, and fixed. They don't even have the appeal of sport, which is that even when one team is much better than the other, you never know for sure what's going to happen next, and nor do the players. By five o'clock all the probabilities could be overturned. And cricket, which allows for the influence of an almost infinite number of variable factors within its Byzantine structure—even I can see this—has class. Alan watching cricket is Alan watching the ants track across the patio, choosing one and following its crazy course, choosing another.

Boredom is what Selwyn has now, and has had for the past year. He lies on his bed with his arm across his forehead like some pallid Victorian poet dying of consumption or permanent writer's block. He can't even be bothered to flush the loo, because that tempestuous cascade of water that sends your turds spinning like upturned boats no longer holds any interest. He avoids me, he doesn't meet my eyes. Boredom is what he drags around with him, parades, wears like a suit of armor. Blank eyes, or eyes rolled upwards in disgust. Slack stance, grudging walk. Where he's headed he doesn't seem to know or care, any forward movement just an excuse to kick aside a Coke can or bottle that happens to be in his path. You wouldn't want him on your team: he's not interested in playing any game, still less in being any good at it. He is, Alan would say, out of form: his shambling, angst-ridden trudge is exactly that of a batsman who keeps missing the ball or hitting it straight to a fielder, or that gangly bowler who can't even throw the ball—not that difficult, surely—in the right direction.

And if being *in* form—your body brimming with life and confidence, alert to everything around you, your timing spot-on and your jokes all funny—equates with being in love, then Selwyn has clearly fallen out of love. With me. He no longer chases me around the kitchen with a water pistol, or puts grapes in my cup of tea. He doesn't ask me where rain comes from, or why you can't pee and sneeze at the same time. He no longer rushes to my bed on my birthday clutching a hand-made card with a sellotaped pop-up frog that falls out when I open it— instead, he dutifully proffers a shop-bought card with 'love' in some fancy typeface that mocks the real thing. I have become a type and not an individual, a representative of a category, an off-the-peg mother.

I HAVE A déjà vu. As I am telling the loss-adjuster that Selwyn has phoned and is safe, as the loss-adjuster is reaching to draw the curtains more closed—either because he doesn't want anyone else except me to see him naked, or to reduce the glare of sunlight on the TV screen—it suddenly comes to me that I have lived this moment before: this room, this light, this exact stance or posture of this exact man with his grey-streaked hair, his so-so stomach, his tortuous knees, shelf of his hip, wit of his eyes, spread of his hands, with this exact distance between us.

It cannot be. It passes.

And then, as he bends to switch off the TV, it comes again—not so sharp, more an echo, a confusion. The Indians are batting again, as they did two days ago and surely they have had their turn?

'Second innings,' says the loss-adjuster. 'They bat, the others bat, then the first lot again.'

'*Again?*'

'Five days . . . '

'And again and again?'

'Just twice.'

'Oh, so it's like that play by Samuel Beckett.' Except that you can see the Beckett in one evening.

This changes everything. It's not like life at all, unless you believe in reincarnation.

You get a *second chance*.

Everything you did wrong first time round you can now do right.

Or vice versa. But different, anyway.

MATCH ANALYSIS, BRIEFLY continued.

. . . Or—to the contrary—Selwyn is out of form because *I* don't love *him* enough.

But I do. If he'd let me.

God, that's weak. Agnieszka is right: *if* clauses are tricky and best avoided, there's something shifty about the whole mix of tenses. It's hardly Selwyn's fault that I happen to have fallen in love with someone else, which does tend to change the focus of one's attention. That I've suddenly changed from being a dependable work-horse bowler into a flash devil-may-care batter. That *I've* become the adolescent, and he quite rightly isn't too happy about being asked if he'd mind being understanding and worldly-wise and middle-aged.

Confusion all round. Which is why I'm groping for something to hold on to, and for some reason fix on a

THE RULES OF PLAY

memory of Selwyn aged about seven eating a plate of spaghetti, the sauce all over his face and the long white strands looping from his mouth. And then I think of spaghetti Westerns, and then cowboys and Indians, and I feel a sudden huge sorrow for the Indians, who had everything stacked against them and were never allowed to win.

'HERE?'

'Further out. Stop—yes, there.'

'And now?'

'Closer.'

It's as if he knows already. He has, I admit, a natural talent. You move in, I remember, with the bowler, a few paces, alert.

'I'm—'

'Yes.'

'You know, seeing you're left-handed, maybe we should change—'

'We could—'

We do. Continuous movement, the full repertoire of classic strokes along with some improvised ones too, unhurried. We are finding, or stumbling upon, new positions. Fine leg. Gully—gully is good. Slip and slip and slip. Deep backward. There are muscles and other bits being exercised I never knew I had. Some of these positions may be structurally unsafe but surely this is how technology advances—the cantilever bridge, new techniques of drilling for oil.

Afterwards, I look at the map of positions that Alan made for me, the star chart. So many of the points are clustered around the narrow strip at the center which he has shaded in. I find a pen on the loss-adjuster's desk and start to join up the dots.

THIS LITTLE, LITTLE place, no room to swing a bat, the size of a generous grave: the lift, in which I go up to my lover and down from my lover. It is modern, functional, smooth, with a dull shine to its surfaces. Sometimes, when I enter, there's a smell trapped in the air, the spoor of a previous occupant; more rarely, there's another occupant in person, and we scan each other in a practiced way, wary but not unfriendly, like dogs passing; the glance I give myself in the mirror is more knowing but not more intimate or lingering. I press the button for 4 or for G, and there's a little *ping* as the lift arrives—a tiny coming, a mini-orgasm, yes, but what it reminds me of more strongly is the bell that sounds at the fairground stall where you test your muscles by striking with a hammer. (Then get to choose your prize: a bow and arrow, or an inflatable parrot. The bow and arrow.) In the order of things my passage in this lift barely registers—it's like the lumbering plod or nonchalant stroll of a batsman from the pavilion to the field of play, and later back again, not a part of the game itself—but nowhere else do I feel more observed, even if only by myself.

In the street, checking my watch, heading towards the Tube station, no one watches me at all, even though this walking-upright business is something I seem to need to re-learn. I have spent so much time horizontal— and yes, on all fours—that I think I may be evolving backwards. My legs are loose; they have forgotten how to support me. Between them (I am grinning like a six-year-old going down a water slide, I know I am) I can feel the loss-adjuster still inside me.

SELWYN HASN'T COME home yet. Or has come and gone. The emptiness of the house is almost tangible; certainly more substantial than I feel myself to be. Somewhere a clock ticks, and the silver disk on the electricity meter slowly revolves. But I don't need the excuse of checking to see in which bedroom a light has been left on: today I am an invisible intruder—even the cat coiled on its chair doesn't trouble to open its eyes—and have a ghost's licence.

Selwyn's room: a mess. But at least it was *his* mess, before I started making my semi-automatic attempt to tidy up on Friday night. Now the mess is no one's. It's as if—which is odd, because I didn't feel this when no one knew where he was, so why should I feel it when I do know?—he's already moved out, gone off into the life he's suddenly discovered is his own, and what's left is just the brittle casing of his time as caterpillar.

Natural wastage. Butterfly now, seeking only to feed and mate. Or moth, crashing against a 60-watt lightbulb.

On to Agnieszka's room, where I haven't been since the night six months ago when I could bear the sound of her sobbing no longer and went in to comfort her, pre-pared—looking forward—to jointly wail against the perfidiousness of men, only to find that the cause of the upset was her college tutor's suggestion that she should delay taking some exam until later in the year. Then it was dark, and I saw nothing; now it is bright, the light through the Velux window good enough to take photographs by. And indeed this room, exactly as it is, could be featured in *House & Garden* or *The World of Interiors*. The bed has been made by the chambermaid of the year; the textbooks and work folders have been arranged by an efficient PA; even the make-up, the tweezers, the tampons, the intimate stuff, looks as if it's straight from the shop, placed by the props manager. Clothes are in cupboards, knick-knacks in rows, God's in his Heaven / All's right with the world! How do those lines go on? Something about 'the bats' sleek sisterhoods.'

This outpost of order and discipline, sealed against the surrounding chaos, is, I imagine, like a missionary's hut in Africa. She civilized, we godless. But there is so little evidence of Agnieszka herself, barely even—I stand still and inhale—the scent of her. And then I am surprised by a framed photograph, of Agnieszka and Selwyn on skateboards in the park, her hand on his shoulder to stop him from falling. It was taken years ago; Selwyn looks about eight or nine; and it's not the photograph itself that surprises me—grazed knees and joy-and-terror in the park are worth remembering—but where it is: not among the ones on the dresser of brothers and dogs and mum and dad in what looks like an underground drinking-den—but by her bed. Before sleep and dreams, the last thing she sees.

Traditionally, it is the father of the house who sleeps with the au pair, who then gets fired. But there is also the other tradition, which I have been blind to—perhaps Selwyn is right, when he says I still think of him as a child and always will—of the maidservant who gets pregnant by the son. Again she gets fired. But this is not the same thing at all.

Which doesn't mean, I tell myself, it's going to happen, let alone happening right now. Because my father died of coronary heart disease I probably have an above-average chance of going the same way, but it doesn't mean I *will*; in fact I'm much more likely to fall off a cliff or stumble under a bus because I'm thinking of words to describe the way the loss-adjuster smells instead of looking where I'm going. And if I try to picture Agnieszka in bed with Alan, or Selwyn, or both of them, it becomes ridiculous. Alan is too sane, Selwyn too stubborn, Agnieszka's taste in men too eccentric. Those permutations are about as plausible as me leading England's bowling attack in their next cricket match. They may be templates of some kind but they're definitely not one-size-fits-all. And the same goes for that even older story that Dr Freud liked so much. So much is contingent, up in the air; if Oedipus had slept with his mother *first*, rather than waiting till his father was out of the way, things might have turned out differently.

The loss-adjuster, I think, will have something to say about Oedipus. In fact we could go through the whole book of classical myths and legends together, rewriting the endings. In the meantime I decide I need tea, or a drink.

On the way downstairs I see that the door to the other bedroom, the bedroom I still share with Alan, is open. I close it.

While the kettle is boiling in the kitchen I retrieve from the oven Selwyn's plate of chicken and beans, which has been there since Friday night, and scrape the congealed orange mess into the bin. As I bend I'm aware of the stern, yellow, Old Testament presence of *Wisden* on the worktop, looking over my shoulder. *The Lord thy God is a jealous God.*

It's two o'clock. Except that Agnieszka told me to be home at this time, and I am, and nothing is happening, it's numbers that hold the world together, if sometimes a bit loosely. If I shop for some gloves I expect most of them to come in pairs and with five fingers for each hand, and the temperature can't be minus 50 degrees Celsius or I wouldn't be out shopping at all. Two plus two does equal four, otherwise the supermarket could be delivering three radishes and forty-nine packets of rolled oats and charging me £798 and I'd have no cause for complaint. Any one number is what it is because of other numbers—they hang together, so that in the end E does equal $mc2$ and we walk upright and most of the time we don't have to think about them. It's when they don't hang together—5,000 hungry people fed by five loaves and two fishes, with twelve baskets of leftovers—that we need to start worrying.

I take it on trust that someone has checked all the numbers in *Wisden* with a calculator and that they do hang together, but the sheer number of numbers in these pages is terrifying. This is a parallel universe in which good and bad, heroism and solid worth, are defined numerically. Also-rans don't get a look-in, the 'criteria for inclusion' being 15,000 runs, 1,000 wickets, 500 'achieved dismissals,' or 10,000 runs *and* 500 wickets, or . . . Divinities include the ones with most runs (B. C. Lara, West Indies, 131—232—6—11,953—400—52.88—34—48—164: presumably the biggest number) and most wickets (S. K. Warne, Australia, 145—40,705—1,761—17,995—708—25.41—871—37—10—57.4—2.65: take your pick). A man called G. Allott squeaks in because he managed to score 0 runs in 101 minutes. There are thousands upon thousands of numbers here, and I am becoming dizzy. If I take just one of them away, will they all come tumbling down? Like G. Allott, I much prefer my numbers in small quantities, or even singly, like grapes. Such as the apparently random but unarguably exact numbers which Selwyn once recited from some off-the-wall website: the age of the youngest pope (eleven), the number of spiders eaten by a human being over the course of a life (eight), the number of newborn children given each day to the wrong parents (twelve).

Two-thirty, and just when I've noticed that the cat has gone from its chair and am thinking I may have shut it in the bedroom when I closed the door and it will pee on the bed, Agnieszka rushes through the door, grabs me by the hand and leads me out to the car. Alan is already there, in the driving seat, and I sit beside him. He is wearing that expression he has for when we are late and it's my fault—even though, this time, it *isn't* my fault—which is entirely different from the one he has for when it's his fault. From behind, Agnieszka places a scarf around my eyes and ties it tightly. I am being kidnapped. I wonder how much ransom they will demand, how much the loss-adjuster will pay to get me back.

It's not unpleasant, being driven blindfold, sealed in my unknowing, though I'm sure it would be different if anyone other than Alan was driving. If we are seen by anyone we know, he is sure to have some thoroughly plausible explanation. I have been training my eyes to count bricks, and have overdone it. I have been staring too long at the sun.

Maybe twenty minutes later we stop, and the scarf is untied. We have arrived at the park, a place I haven't been since the days of grazed knees. Another whole generation is here, with their high-spec turbo-charged buggies and their curious hairstyles and their colorful new vernacular. They are waving at me.

'This is Tomas, this is Alessandra, this is Marek, this is Jadwiga, this is Gino, this is Fang,' says Agnieszka. And this, hanging behind the others as if he's trying to avoid me, is Harvey.

As we all walk towards an open green space, herded by Agnieszka, enlightenment dawns. One of these people is carrying the plastic bag with the bat and wooden sticks. Wickets, I mean. Or stumps. Alan is tossing a red ball so it spins in the air and catching it with one hand. He has the same glint in his eye as when he sees a bottle of good red wine being uncorked.

Very reluctantly, and only after I point out that there are many tiny children within hitting range, and might even be seagulls too, Agnieszka agrees that we play not with Alan's hard red ball but with an old tennis ball that I remember as being in the boot of the car. It's a visual memory: the ball is wedged between a carton of motor oil and a Wellington boot, and has been there since time immemorial, waiting for this very occasion. The question of teams takes longer to resolve; eventually, after dismissing women against men and five against five, we decide everyone is to bat individually, in turn. Except that I am not allowed either to bat or to bowl or even to run, because I, having read *Wisden*, am the umpire.

It is fun, almost. It might even be wisdom, almost. If Selwyn were here and if the loss-adjuster were here it would be both.

I have no idea what I'm doing, but I do know I'm wearing the wrong shoes. I stand behind the stumps, which I thought would give me some protection but doesn't, because the batter is facing me and not at all far away. Every so often I hold up both my hands or use one hand to make a sort of scattering motion, like sowing seeds, like I've seen the umpires do on TV. Agnieszka applauds; for her I can do no wrong. But when they all shout and look towards me to decide if the batter's turn is over, I can do no right. I decide to do it alternately, which seems fair: the first time I pretend I haven't heard anything, the next time I hold up one finger, the next time I pretend, etc.

It's not easy, being an umpire, even after I've kicked off my shoes. On the other hand I could, if I wanted, make them all play while standing on one leg—rule 347, paragraph C—and they'd have to obey me.

Alan is seriously trying not to take this seriously. He chases the ball hard and throws it back very accurately and when the person he's throwing to ducks under it he grins sheepishly—odd expression: do sheep grin?—as if it's all his own fault. Which it might be. But really I think that grin is worth ten runs, or more.

There is, of course, a large and excited dog who believes that the ball is entirely its own, and from whose mushy jaws only Alessandra seems capable of retrieving it.

Fang—or Feng—is the all-time star. I never knew they played cricket in China. He runs, he catches, he hits, he shows Jadwiga how to hold the bat, he bowls very slowly to Alessandra and very fast to Marek, he rushes off to the café to get Cokes at half-time (half-time?), he is everywhere. He will go far. I wonder who his mother is, and what she knows. Agnieszka and Feng, I think. Feng and Agnieszka. But neither shows any interest in the other.

Everyone is laughing, sweating, exclaiming; there is a fellowship here that, even though most of us have only known each other for one hour, might allow for the exchange of the most private secrets. And then it is all brought to a sudden end, arrested, aborted, by guess who. Harvey, who for most of the afternoon has been as invisible as a man his size is capable of being, stumbles after the ball and stops short, wheezing. His face turns beet-root, his eyes bulge, his arms flap wildly around him as if he is a bird that can't fly but hasn't been told. He is hyperventilating.

Agnieszka takes his hand and tells him to breathe deeply. He closes his eyes, like someone who is preparing to make some grim but unavoidable announcement, and then opens them wide as if expecting it to be another day. He is indecently grateful. I pray to God, cruelly, that he is not telling Agnieszka that he loves her.

Feng calls an ambulance but by the time it has arrived Alan and Agnieszka have bundled Harvey into the car and themselves driven to the hospital. I am over-apologetic to the ambulance crew, who seem to regard me as personally responsible for the waste of their time, the obstruction at the park gate, the traffic congestion throughout west London, and having to work on a Sunday afternoon. I sit on the grass with Feng, Marek, Gino, Jadwiga and Tomas. Alessandra has disappeared, I think with the owner of the enthusiastic dog. We are a team, we depend on one another. Tomas wants to play football. Feng attempts to teach us an alternative and much simpler form of cricket called French cricket, though no one knows why. I am good at this, because my legs are thin.

THERE'S STILL A throbbing pain in my hip where I fell last night in the cupboard but I know now why I married Alan. Because Selwyn was under-age. It wasn't Alan I fell in love with but Selwyn. There is nothing selfish or sly or malicious or capricious about Alan—he is, as they say, especially when they're choosing a new captain for the team, a safe pair of hands—but it was Selwyn who bowled me over. After years of working my guts out at this thing called human relationships, he taught me how to play.

WE USED TO play in the park, hide-and-seek. He wouldn't close his eyes, or he'd skip numbers when he was counting to a hundred. So would I, sometimes. And a kind of kick-ball, never my favorite.

We used to play draughts on his bed, and whenever he was about to lose he'd wriggle his feet and upset the board.

We used to play in the kitchen. Because Alan supports Chelsea we made him a supper in which every item of food was blue. We once managed to bake a chocolate cake with a pencil-sharpener inside it.

We used to play in the bathroom, with funnels and jugs, and making cave-paintings on the walls with washable ink (do *not* trust the label).

We used to play in the swimming pool. 'Can you touch the bottom?' Going under water isn't natural, you have to learn to do it. There are two ways: either you breathe out before you go under, pushing all the air out your lungs that would otherwise keep you on the surface, or you breathe in first and then out as you go down, the air rushing upwards in a trail of bubbles. Then you can sit on the floor of the pool, watching the other bodies moving slowly around you without knowing which is which, who is who.

We used to play on buses, making up rude rhymes, showing off.

In any place where we were together, we used to play: arm-wrestling (his propped on a fat book), not-blinking competitions, nonsense languages.

We used to play.

SOMEWHERE NEAR UR, on the plains of Mesopotamia 5,000 years ago, a bored young goat-herd starts chucking a stone at some object on the ground a few yards away—another stone, or a pile of them, or the Mesopotamian equivalent of an old Coke can. Some mangled piece of hardware left behind by an invading army. Boys do this—watch them on a pebbly beach. The bored goat-herd's bored companion picks up an old thigh-bone that happens to be lying around and uses it to hit away the first goat-herd's stone before it can knock over the Coke can.

This goes on for some time. Up above, two birds are swooping and circling—buzzards maybe, or vultures. The sun beats down. When the second goat-herd hits the stone far away he's happy, and the first goat-herd is annoyed. When the first goat-herd's stone strikes the Coke can, it's his turn to hit—*smite*—with the thigh-bone.

'No!' shouts the first goat-herd at one point. 'That would have hit! You're not allowed to get your leg in the way!'

At another point, fed up with running to fetch the stone that has been hit by the second goat-herd, the first goat-herd goes to the foot of the scree and brings back a little stock of stones clutched in both hands. There happen to be six of them. But this is just wishful thinking.

A wolf creeps up and snatches one of the goats. The two boys are so absorbed in their game that they don't even notice, don't even hear the dying goat's gurgle as the wolf chomps into its neck.

The farmer sacks the goat-herds. He puts an ad in the *Ur Gazette*: 'Wanted, two goat-herds. Must have no imagination.'

Friday | Saturday | Sunday | **Monday** | Tuesday

*W*hen I'm in front of him I don't know because I just see *him*, but in profile he looks like a doctor. A good one, who has spent years studying the human body and learning all the Latin names and which drug companies offer the best freebies without ever losing his sense of wonder. His face is lined; he looks older than Alan although in fact is younger. He has lived in cities and survived on little sleep. He listens, and I feel he is thinking of possibilities, and then discounting some and refining others, but never hurrying towards a conclusion because that would not be listening. He notices things: that I don't like making decisions that require thinking about; the scar below my right ankle where I was bitten as a child by a Spanish dog that might have had rabies (and I waited years for the dormant symptoms to announce themselves, being almost disappointed when they didn't because the dog was then reduced to the most commonplace and mean-ingless of dogs—until, that is, this man noticed the scar). And his listening and noticing are far more than just professional: as a builder who also happens to paint watercolors at the weekend, for instance, will see cracks in a wall and the crumbling mortar but also the stains, the patterns of discoloration, the lines of the cables snak-ing slackly down, the shadows. In the end he will say, regarding any possible treatment, that this is the situa-tion and we could do this or do that or perhaps just wait to see how it develops, and which way would I like to go? So I choose, but really I feel that he has made the choice for me. I trust him: not always to be right, but to have knowledge of what is good.

I did know a builder once—well, a plumber—who loved music. He promised himself that when he retired he'd learn to play the piano. And then when he did retire his fingers were too stiff and calloused. This story makes me shudder; it's like one of those creepy fables for chil-dren with animals that speak and a moral instruction from some right-wing party manifesto tagged on at the end.

Now the loss-adjuster is concentrating, because a white van has just cut in front of him and the traffic is heavy and he is looking out for the names of streets, not having driven this way before. He picked me up at the gypsy's Tube station; we are driving to Southall, to a warehouse that has burnt down and that he has to write a report on, and I, to all appearances, am his secretary or PA or, being hardly dressed for the office, his mistress or concubine.

Unlikely partnerships may flourish, as between a top-order batsman and an incompetent one who may on rare occasions play out of his skin and frustrate the bowlers, who believe he has no right to survive.

Southall is little India with red London buses—saris, sweets, bangles, box upon box of yellow mangos for sale on the pavements and the green doors of the Methodist Church in the King's Hall boarded up, its windows grey with dust, its congregation having long since taken flight. The music coming through the open windows of a car stopped next to us at a traffic light is jaunty and breezy and full of little skippy rhythms, and for a moment I feel as if we've arrived in a warmer, more colorful place where none of the old rules apply. But then we turn through the open gates of a small industrial park and there, waiting to greet us at the smoke-blackened door of his Fashion Fabrics warehouse, is Mr Chidambaram in a baggy brown suit with trousers that puddle round his feet.

The loss-adjuster puts on a pair of bright yellow Wellington boots and a matching yellow hard hat, the type that builders wear on construction sites. He looks mock-heroic, which suits him. Mr Chidambaram—tiny beside the loss-adjuster, and old and grey and unshaven with the worry of what he's been through—rolls up his trouser legs to reveal shiny black shoes and spindly but very hairy shins. Together, Don Quixote and Sancho Panza, they trudge through the wasteland that was once a treasure-house of brightly colored cloths and silks and polyesters, although truly there is not much to see: tangled metal bars, black heaps of sodden and unidentifiable material, shards of glass from the empty window frames. I watch from the doorway, breathing in a stench of drenched cinders that almost makes me retch. The loss-adjuster's yellow boots make immaculate ridged prints on the ash-covered floor.

After the tour of the warehouse-that-was, we enter the door of an adjacent office-type building, climb a flight of concrete steps, walk down a corridor and enter a room that appears to be a dressing room: there are rows of saris on racks, as if for a chorus of Indian dancers, and also a long bench against one wall, a low round table, a calendar advertising a driving school ('male and female instructors') and a TV hanging from a metal bracket. The walls and ceiling are painted pink, the pink a child might choose to paint the flesh of white English people, although if I really was that color I'd surely be in hospital, in an isolation ward. And here, on cue, is a child, a young girl, sitting cross-legged on the floor watching the TV. India are still batting, nudging past 300, taking control of the whole game. Mrs Chidambaram is here too, a large woman wrapped in vivid turquoise emerging from behind the saris. She wants me to sit beside her on the bench, so I do, and she smiles happily and pats my knee. And the men go out.

The loss-adjuster turns as he goes through the doorway, waves his yellow hard hat apologetically in my direction and offers a smile that's more of a shrug. They are going to talk about money, I know. Insurance policies and accounts sheets and invoices and receipts are going to be taken out of filing cabinets and arranged on the desk in Mr Chidambaram's office. There will be a cracking of finger knuckles, a chewing of betel leaves, a nodding and a shaking of heads, confusing if you don't know the code. Enormous sums will be spoken aloud, with seeming casualness. Calculators will be tapped with quick fingers—more numbers, glowing green, added and subtracted and divided. I have an impulse to go to that room and remind the loss-adjuster that I speak Spanish, but perhaps I am better off here.

I tell Mrs Chidambaram that she must be going

through a terrible time, with the burning down of the warehouse, but either she doesn't speak any English or she doesn't want to talk to me. Fair enough. The child, however, who is called Jeevita, speaks fluent and wonderfully exact English, and is happy to tell me about her pet rabbit, about another warehouse in north London that's owned by her uncle, and how Sachin Tendulkar is the best batsman in the world and India will win.

Us three women—we are a mini-harem, in the privacy of our own quarters. And yet all the time I sit here I am strongly aware of the presence, or absence, of men. It's as if, although I'm not cold in the slightest, some man has insisted on lending me his jacket and has draped it around my shoulders.

The only visible men in this room are the ones on the TV screen, doing their stuff. And this remains, however happy they are to explain it and beam at me when I clap at the right times, *their* stuff. The language—the restrictive code—with all its hallowed jargon; the overload of statistics; the undying heroes of ancient days; the smell of linseed oil, and of the liniments and lotions they slather all over their bristly skin; the locker-room jokes and guffaws; the bruises worn as badges; the bonding from schooldays to prime and beyond. The *innocence*, the Golden Age: the boys off together on a merry school trip, without girls to distract or confuse or terrify them. The baggy white trousers are not unattractive (and surely more convenient for nursing an erection than crotch-hugging Lycra)—but who washes them and irons the creases?

Oh, but it's something—isn't it?—to stand stock-still in the middle of a field as a hard leather ball hurtles towards you at 90 miles per hour. With only a thin strip of wood to fend it off; with only a metal bar screwed to your helmet to protect your eyes, pads over your shins and a plastic triangle around your genitals. *At the going down of the sun and in the morning.* Something foolish, willful, show-off, as well as brave, but something. Something Alan will pay to watch, and innumerable others of his and lesser ilk: the desk-bound, the bar-huggers, the weary addicts, the paunchy fantasists.

Four! V. V. Laxman cracks the ball across the grass to the rope, and holds his pose for half a second longer than he needs to. Left foot ranged forward, steely-eyed, all the angles of his body in perfect balance, he could be carved in stone on a pedestal in the capital city, alongside the gods and the liberators.

MRS CHIDAMBARAM HAS gone, vanished. Not even a pat on my knee in farewell. The players come off the field for lunch: India are 316 for 5. I ask Jeevita if Indian women play cricket and she is full of information. The captain of the Indian women's team is Mithali Raj. She scored 214 runs against England in Somerset in 2002. She trained as a classical dancer. She works for the railways.

A sudden hollow gapes in the pit of my stomach: praising this unknown other woman, Jeevita's eyes shine with an impossibly eager brightness.

Then a scurry of activity is happening around me. Jeevita's mother calls her name from somewhere distant— a harsh, peremptory voice—and the girl rushes out; the loss-adjuster and Mr Chidambaram walk into the room and smile down at me in approval of my good behavior; Jeevita returns with cushions, throws them on the floor, and dashes away; and finally Jeevita comes back through the door with her mother, both bearing trays with large plastic beakers and plates of food.

We take off our shoes and sit cross-legged on the floor around the table and eat. Mr Chidambaram's trousers are rolled up even further than before, exposing knees that resemble gnarled and knotted firewood. The beakers contain sugary mango juice. On the plates are sweets: slabs of lime green and orange and pale brown, red whorls, black balls flecked with white. Mrs Chidambaram ruthlessly force-feeds me, insisting I have at least one of everything. Afterwards, Jeevita brings hot wet towels for our hands. As we leave, the players are coming back onto the field.

'DO YOU THINK —'
    'No.'
    'That I'd make a good loss-adjuster's companion?'
    'Consort?'
    'Even better.'
    'Oh yes. I've known this for some time. Since Edinburgh. When you come into a room, people think they've gained something, whatever they've lost.'
    'And have they?'
    I'm not used to compliments, and they're nice. They're an underused genre. The cricket commentators use them all the time—'That was beautifully bowled,' 'He plays that stroke better than anyone else in the game today'—but not face-to-face. Do cricketers blush?
    Now I have something to live up to. It's like having a new job.
    The loss-adjuster's eyes stay on the road ahead. We are driving back into London, the landmarks becoming more standardized as the city jerks by in a series of road-works and traffic lights: Tescos, Boots, signs to leisure centers. I put my hand on his thigh.

'What did you think I was asking, when you said no?'

He has to track back. 'I was thinking you were asking about Mr Chidambaram, whether he's going to get all the insurance he's claiming. And the answer, probably, is no. At least, it's unlikely.'

And the loss-adjuster explains, which is a different genre entirely. The insurance on Mr Chidambaram's Fashion Fabrics has been organized by his brother, who has his own warehouse and a number of policies arranged through a broker who is a family friend. The premiums seem to have been paid regularly by Mr Chidambaram, but somewhere on the route through the brother and the broker there have been, you could say, delays, and the money hasn't always gone through to the insurance company.

I almost wish I hadn't asked. I didn't ask, actually: the question I did ask was about me. This could mean the end of Mr Chidambaram's livelihood; it could mean that Jeevita will never have a chance to play cricket for India, or for England. And whatever I can mumble about extended families and support networks will sound callous.

'Can't you fix it?'

'I'll do what I can.'

'It's your job.'

'I don't bring things back. I don't *make good*. I adjust—so that the outcome, I hope, is one that everyone believes to be fair. Given the circumstances.'

'You mean it's all about money, and numbers—add a bit here, subtract a bit there?' It doesn't seem very much. Whatever the circumstances.

'In the end, yes.'

'And there are laws and rules you have to stick to?'

'Of course.'

'So for example, it really makes no difference if what I've lost is something I don't really care about, something I'd forgotten I even had, or something that means everything to me? It's just about market value?'

The loss-adjuster drives onto a garage forecourt, past the petrol pumps, and stops near the machine where you check your tire pressures. And adjust them, if necessary. He tells me I probably don't want to know this, which is true, but let's talk about his work. For the record. And he goes back into explaining mode, which I had so taken for granted was Alan's, and not this man's, speciality. Yes, personal value, subjective value even, can be counted in—it's the part of the job he enjoys most, talking with people, assessing the impact of what's happened to them and thinking of ways to alleviate it. There are computer programs that help with this. He spends a lot of time on computers, checking policies, working out valuations: desk stuff. In the case of personal injury, there are programs and scales that deal with arms, legs, elbows, fingers—and earlobes, presumably, and testicles and nipples. Two people's knees are not necessarily of equal value. It depends on so many factors: age, income, future prospects, dependants . . . He tells me about people called forensic economists, and asks me what VSL stands for. Not Very Sober Lunch, not Violent Sexual Libido. The Value of a Statistical Life.

The traffic chugs past: cars, white vans, lorries packed with yogurts or roof-tiles or frozen meat. It doesn't *surge* or thunder, it doesn't race by at a speed to set this stationary vehicle rocking. It keeps to the left-hand lane, it obeys the speed limit, more or less.

Idiot. Who does he think he's talking to—some first-year student who shouldn't be on the course anyway?

My hand back on his thigh. What he's saying is simply that he has a job, and like all jobs it's often petty and tedious. He doesn't, for a living, change the world. What he's telling me, I think, is that he's not The One, that there isn't a *One*, that One is just a number, that he's a man among men, innumerable men.

My forehead against his neck, my lips against his chin, awkward, reaching. I may not have had it laid out so plainly before, but it's hardly complicated. What does he think I want? A man among men, yes. Pick a number, any number. This one.

I choose, or am chosen. *And* am chosen.

He looks at me, and puts his arm around me, and I try not to think he is assessing my value, and I notice, I can't help it, that as he turned towards me his trouser legs have ridden up.

I wish this wasn't so. That unwitting exposure. More crude, more revealing, for a man, than his buttons or zip undone. Far more than complete nudity, those two inches of pale taut skin between the top of his socks and the bottom of his trousers make me think of the way of all flesh, and the end of play. And how short the time for play can be. Already those men in white on the green field are younger than me. Already, indeed long ago, for them—if this was not the case they wouldn't be on TV, they wouldn't be representing their country—the game has ceased to be play and become work: a job (no less so than loss-adjusting), routine, day in day out, the days and months and years clocked up. They are professionals, with signed contracts. With all the single-mindedness that implies, and the consequences: stress fractures, broken metatarsals, cruciate ligaments, *groin injuries*—a phrase whose expressive generality suggests some unspecified and lingering STD. Don't take me there.

He switches on the engine and we move back into the traffic.

But it's different. The journey back into London seems to take longer than the journey out. (The opposite, surely, to what's usual: the hours and hours of the drive to Cornwall, Selwyn's 'Are we nearly there?' repeated at least every twenty minutes from the moment we turned right at the end of the street, the missed turn-off on the motorway, the roadworks, the stoppings to pee or to look at the map; and on the way back, the speed towards what is known, the rush to confirm that the cat hasn't forgotten us.) And it's even more different when we get back to the flat. We go up in the lift, standing apart, and into the flat, and there's a new smell, somehow. Cigarettes have been smoked. The TV has been moved into the living room and the figure sitting on the sofa watching it— watching cricket—is Selwyn.

I sort of jump towards him, through the air, and stumble, and the loss-adjuster has to grip my arm.

'Hello, mum,' he says. Just that, neutral.

I can't hug him because he won't stand up, so I sit beside him. I rest my head on his shoulder, this other

THE RULES OF PLAY

man's shoulder, which yields, a bit. It feels the right thing to do, and is.

'How long have you been here?' I ask, quietly, in case it isn't really him.

'I got here last night.'

'You stayed the night here?'

'On the sofa.'

Something stirs within me, uncoiling—a response, a Pavlovian one—and I squash it immediately. Thank God I don't have to ask him if he's got his toothbrush with him, or if he's had any breakfast. We're in a different place, somewhere new, and it's good. Though the old place might be easier.

'Have you—'

He turns towards me, hugs me, to shut me up.

I LOVE HIS scrapy fingernails, and the scar behind his left ear which no hairdresser has seen for over a year. I love the way he used to walk, even when he knew I was watching him, as if no one was watching him and the world was his own, and I even love the way he walks now, which is different when he knows I am watching him. I love his eyes not being any color at all I can put a name to, so that whenever I think about what color they are I have to go and look at them. I love the fact that he breathes in and breathes out for exactly the length of his lifetime, his own and no one else's, no more and no less.

And it turns out I couldn't tell the difference—admittedly at some distance, and on a television screen—between the penis of my own sixteen-year-old boy and that of a thirty-four-year-old trainee accountant.

Who is this boy?

'WHY DIDN'T YOU tell me?' I shout at the loss-adjuster, inches from his face. We are in the kitchen. He is making tea or something equally useless and evasive.

'He said he'd go away if I told you.'

'But why *here*?'

'I think he wanted you to find him here.'

'But this morning, you knew he was here all the time and you never . . . *Why*?'

The kettle has boiled. 'I think—I don't know him well enough, yet—I think he tends to sleep in the mornings. He's sixteen. I do want to, though.'

'Want to what?'

'Know him. Get to know him.'

I look at him, this man I have seen not only naked and aroused but in bright yellow boots and a builder's hat. He is far too calm. He's about to ask me if Selwyn takes sugar and how many.

'No, not *why*.' I do some re-ordering. '*How?*'

The loss-adjuster looks at me blankly, infuriatingly.

'How often, for start?'

'He came yesterday, late afternoon. The first time.'

We look at each other, and I choose to believe him. Even so, Selwyn knew where to come. He must have followed me. How many times? For days. Past the man doing the three-card trick outside the Tube station.

Would I have walked differently if I'd known I was being watched? But I've never believed that this thing I am doing is *wrong*. Not if no one is hurt. So why, if I can look in his math homework book, can't he look in mine, what I do with my days?

Because it was up to me to show him, not for him to spy.

I turn towards the living room. Not once have I ever gone into Selwyn's bedroom without knocking first. I shout, 'Selwyn, you followed me, how could you?'

'If you shout at him,' the loss-adjuster tells me, 'he won't ever want to talk to you, call you up, confide in you.'

'If I don't shout at him,' I shout back, 'he'll never see me as a person in my own right, not just a mother who provides and provides and provides.'

Selwyn is standing in the kitchen doorway. He has

that sheepish—for want of a better word—smile on his face, the one that belongs to Alan too.

'Three sugars, please,' says Selwyn.

'Oh,' says the loss-adjuster. 'No sugar, I'm afraid.'

'I went out and got some. It's in the cupboard over the fridge,' says this boy who *never* puts things away in cupboards.

'You have a *key?*' I demand, or exclaim.

There's a noise from the living room, from the TV. A noise made by several thousand people. We go to look. Pietersen is out for a duck. We watch the replay: Anil Kumble bowling, and Pietersen takes a mighty swipe and the ball flies high, high in the air, up among the seagulls, and straight down into the hands of the fielder at deep square leg. The fielder is mobbed by his gleeful team-mates.

'Idiot!' we say, every one of us, even though Selwyn has never expressed any interest in cricket at all since he was nine years old.

THE SECOND INNINGS, this reincarnation business, is not straightforward. Firstly, you can't wipe the slate clean: whatever mistakes you've made before still count and have to be made up for before you can really start again. Secondly, unless you have a good fitness coach the first innings has left you so exhausted you can hardly lift up the bat. And you become aware of how little time you have left, and the math gets more complicated.

'Do you want anything to eat?' I ask.

The loss-adjuster has gone out, to leave us alone. As if he were an obstacle that we'd have had to talk around or through. I've often wondered what heads of state talk about when they meet in private session, without all their minions and minders: the new Johnny Depp film? The servant problem? If they could only discover some passionate interest or hobby in common—butterflies come to mind—they might save the world.

Selwyn, rightly, ignores my question.

'Why are you here, Selwyn?'

'Why are you here?'

'Because this is the place where a man I love is. Lives.' But I'm not looking at him when I say this, and when I do focus on what I seem to be looking at, it turns out to be a photograph on the wall of the loss-adjuster in some group of other people. Strangers, anniversaries. I chose this man, yes, but I didn't choose to be *here*.

'You mean someone you fuck?'

The prudishness of the young: when Alan, coerced into this, and I took Selwyn to an exhibition at the

Hayward showing how artists have portrayed bodies—anatomy, the nitty-gritty—he backed away, didn't want to know. Or look at; or look at with Alan and me there with him.

'It's a part of life,' I say weakly, and immediately I understand the loss-adjuster's reluctance to explain things—it isn't just laziness—and how explanations so often *get in the way* and yet also may be downright necessary: how else is anyone supposed to work out, or even take an interest in, with no help from outside except maybe a guidebook that's written as if it's been translated into Japanese and then back again, what's going on in the middle of the green field, what the players are doing as they run or hit or throw or stand still or sit with their feet up in the pavilion reading the paper? And why.

'It's a part of *my* life. A good part. It's what I want to do. I enjoy it.'

'Exactly,' he says. '*Your* life. And the rest of us can piss off, so you can have fun.'

'I don't mean that.'

'What *do* you mean?'

'I mean . . . I mean, if I didn't love him, this wouldn't be happening. But it is happening, and it isn't just about me, it's all of us. And nothing, nothing in any of this means that I love you any less than I've always done.'

'So what about Alan?'

Not 'Dad.' We are equals, without being equal. Something has dissolved while I wasn't looking. A family. We have nothing that links us except what we want to link us. I know that's not true.

'It's not something that you seem to be getting much of at the moment,' I say. 'I see that.'

'What isn't?'

'Enjoyment. Fun. Love.'

'How do you know? You don't even know who my friends are, you always get their names wrong.'

'Because I hardly see them for long enough to—'

'Whose fault is that?'

'Mine, probably.'

Circles, round and round. I'm getting dizzy. He's right, it's true there's a lot in his life, now, that I don't know about but surely he doesn't *want* me to know, or maybe he does, but in some magical way that doesn't involve *asking* and *telling*. And now we seem to be playing roles in a Sunday-night TV play and I was never any good at watching those—after the first ten minutes, twenty at most, I'd get confused by the plot, I never knew who was having an affair with who—so how can anyone expect me to be good at being *in* one?

Then Selwyn does something astounding. From

somewhere about himself, as if it's completely habitual, he takes out a cigarette and lights it. With a lighter from his jeans pocket. For a moment, it's like him telling me he's gay. Or has a child. He's sixteen. *Has* he had sex?

'Do you want one?' Offering me the packet.

'No thanks.'

'I know. You don't smoke. But you must have done at some time?'

I nod. It's not heroin.

'Did you stop because of me?'

'I can't remember now.' Oh but I can—the struggle to be virtuous, the feeling that if this was virtue, then let me choose hell. 'But yes, I think partly because of you.'

'Go on, have one.'

I take a cigarette, he lights it for me. I breathe in and almost choke but it's a huge relief, him taking charge.

'He's nice,' he says. 'I like him.'

'Who?'

'The man who lives here. The man you love.' He does that smile, that sheepish grin. 'The man you have sex with. The man you fuck.'

He stands up. He goes to the kitchen—he *lives* here, in this functional, story-book flat, he has slept here a whole night, which I have never done, *which I have never done*—and he brings back a saucer and places it on the table. An ashtray.

Which he uses, nonchalantly, and brings the cigarette back to his mouth, and inhales. 'He says I can work for him. He says there's work I can do.'

And I think: work—Selwyn in a suit? Collar and tie? A haircut.

'You don't believe me, do you?'

'Selwyn, what are you telling me? Do you know what time people get up in the morning, to go to work?'

'Yes. It's like school. I've done it for years. But this is different.'

'What would you do?'

'I don't know. I think I'd find things.'

'Find things to do?'

'No. Find things.'

Car keys—we'd be ready to go out, and Alan couldn't find the car keys, and Selwyn would find them. In the kitchen, where I'd taken the shopping. By the kettle. The tax letter, one of many but this one was crunch, so I lost it, and a day before the deadline—panic—Selwyn walks over to Alan's folder of holiday brochures, those islands we will never get near to, and even if we do we will be stuck in the bank at the airport arguing forever about currency conversion rates, and picks it out. The Gameboy we bought him for his birthday, two months early because of some special offer, and hid it in the drawer where Alan keeps his socks—he found it. The TV remote, almost daily. My credit card, pound coins, Agnieszka's bus pass. He was a child, low center of gravity and close to the ground, where things tend to end up. But maybe, maybe, it was more than that. On a walk in the country he picked a twenty-pound note out of a bush. A natural talent.

'He's a loss-adjuster, isn't he?' Selwyn goes on, with a fine and undeniable logic. 'He explained what that is. Sometimes it's bad, when factories get burned down or cars get smashed, but sometimes he gets called in just because people have lost things. He told me about this woman who—well, I mean, if it's just that, if it's just losing stuff, then I could go and look for it. I'm good at that, finding things.'

A human metal detector.

A gap in the market.

He can do anything, anything in the world, this boy. He could stop wars. He could be the second-youngest pope.

And then the loss-adjuster has returned, and is walking across the room towards me. He kisses me on my forehead and sits down on the sofa, next to Selwyn.

Why, whenever there are three people, does it always have to be two against one?

I stub out my cigarette on the saucer. It was horrible. I say, 'I should go home.'

Strange word: 'home' is where Selwyn is, and Alan, but if Selwyn is here . . . The other place seems very far away, and much longer ago than this morning.

I'm not expecting to be contradicted, and no one does.

'Are you coming with me?' I ask Selwyn.

'If you're going home, yes.' He doesn't get up.

'Where else would we be going?'

'I mean, if you're going home.'

Oh. He means, of course, a woman's, a mother's, place: home, and not ever to come to this flat again. But right now, which is exactly the time I should be having this argument, I'm suddenly too tired. I know there's something I should be fighting for but the focus is blurred.

I get my bag. Now Selwyn stands up and seems to be waiting but there's nothing to wait for. I put my arm around his stiff, sharp shoulders, as sharp and as hard as that thing I fell against in the cupboard beneath the stairs, and we head for the door.

The loss-adjuster offers to drive us and I say no, no,

we're fine, without even turning to look at him, and already we're standing by the lift, waiting for it to arrive. But now there's a heaviness, a sluggishness, encasing us, the lift torpid and pompous, its light yellow and old, time slowing down, and to shake this off I start walking, as soon as we come out of the door to the street, faster than usual. Selwyn strides to keep up.

And then, suddenly, I'm aware he's no longer beside me, and I turn.

He's standing at the edge of the pavement. A party of teenage foreign backpackers threads between us, their voices loud and carefree—Spanish, my other language. He's forgotten something, I think. We'll have to do this all over again.

'Actually,' Selwyn says, 'I think I'll hang around for a bit.'

Okay. He'll follow, in his own time.

'I mean,' he says, 'I'm going back to the flat.'

That sheepish smile. And then he's walking away, walking back. He has a key. He puts things in cupboards.

I HAVE A pounding headache, not nagging but bully-ing, despotic. I have been force-fed with deep-fried sugar for lunch, I have been messed around by Selwyn whom I love, I think, and I have smoked my first cigarette in ten years. *Of course* I have a headache. As soon as I get home I walk upstairs to the bathroom, ignoring Agnieszka's attempt to detain me, and take down a box of painkillers from the shelf in the cabinet. I sit on the edge of the bath and read the small print on the back of the box. *More common side effects may include: abnormal dreams, abnormal ejaculation, abnormal vision, anxiety, diminished sex drive, dizziness, dry mouth, flu-like symptoms, flushing, gas, headache, impotence, insomnia, itching, loss of appetite, nausea, nervousness, occasional forgetfulness, rash, sinusitis, sleepiness, sore throat, sweating, tremors, upset stomach, vomiting. Less common side effects may include: bleeding problems, chills, confusion, ear pain, emotional instability, fever, frequent urination, high blood pressure, loss of memory, palpitations, sleep disorders, weight gain, vertigo. In children and adolescents, less common side effects may also include: excessive menstrual bleeding, hyperactivity, mania or hypomania, nosebleeds, personality changes.*

I chuck the box in the bin. I decide I am feeling better.

ALAN IS IN the kitchen, in darkness. He must know I'm here, but he doesn't turn round. What he's doing, I gradually realize, is rearranging the recipe books on the shelf beside the cooker in alphabetical order. By author, or title? He reaches up—he has short arms, whenever he buys a new jacket he has to get the sleeves shortened—and brings down a book, and examines its cover, and reaches up again to place it back on the shelf in a different place. Again and again. It's like an improvised performance in a small room above a pub, one the actor doesn't know how to bring to an end. But that's okay. Although I'd like to know what happens next I'm also happy just watching, leaning against the doorframe. I've paid for my ticket.

Then he sits down, still without turning on the light. It's possible that he too is training his eyes, to see in the dark. I want him to tell me what he sees.

Before that, Agnieszka must update me. She is ironing in the bathroom at the top of the stairs. '*Fffshhhh*,' she has said, while I was watching Alan, imitating the noise of the iron. And now she is singing. Calling me.

The trip to the hospital with Harvey was an anticlimax: they put him on a nebulizer, gave him a prescription and sent him home. And last night Harvey took Agnieszka to a musical in the West End. She laughs and waves her arms around as she tells me about the dance routines and the special effects, and I suggest she switches off the iron before she knocks it over. Then she laughs even more when she tells how Harvey got annoyed and told her that what they were watching was moving and tragic. I am not enjoying hearing this. It's clear that Harvey's all-round blockheadedness is exactly what's making Agnieszka very fond of him.

After the musical he took her to a hotel, a Hilton hotel.

'So he's rich, Agnieszka? That helps.'

Agnieszka is not sure. 'He pays with tickets, like at the theatre.'

'And then?'

'We go to room, drink champagne.' She screws up her nose.

'Not good?' I have sat down at the top of the stairs. I am tired. Agnieszka is standing behind the ironing board with hands far apart, like Manet's woman behind the bar at the Folies-Bergère. Agnieszka is no less formidable.

'Not fizzy. Not cold.' She clearly expected more from a hotel calling itself the Hilton.

'There are two beds, thin ones,' she goes on, 'but bouncy. You know?'

I can guess. She tried them out. She sat, or maybe even lay, on the mattress, and bounced up and down. She's a practical girl.

'He kisses me, then he tries to move these beds to make one big bed. I am wanting to help but he says no, so only I am watching. His face gets red. I am worried, I am trying again to help, he pushes me away. He makes this noise, like in the park?'

I wheeze, putting a lot of exaggeration into it. It comes surprisingly easily, as if a small animal inside me is trying to come out. 'Wheeze,' I say, drawing breath.

'Yes, wheeze. He wheezes, but worse than in the park. He starts to make like the bird again—'

'You mean his arms?'

'Waving, like the seagull on the ground, when it starts to fly.' She demonstrates.

'I tell him to lie down, breathe like this.' More demonstration, and this time I join in. Slow, deep breaths: in, out, in, out.

'He has some pills in his jacket, I find them.'

'Oh, Agnieszka.'

'We lie down, very quiet. The pills make him better. After some time he tells me he must take these pills every day but he doesn't, they make his skin very bad.' She scratches her forearm.

'Yes, scratchy. A rash.'

'One time, he says, he went to psychology—psychology something.'

'Therapist. It's easier.'

'This woman, she ask him why he thinks everything so dangerous, why he must be punished, what he done wrong? But really, Harvey has done nothing wrong, ever.'

She shakes her head. 'So one time is it, he doesn't go to see this woman again.'

'No,' I say, after a pause. I stand and hug Agnieszka awkwardly, over the ironing board. But she stiffens, resists, the Communist poster-girl again, determined. She doesn't cry. She's not going to let me off so easily.

Because it's true I've been remiss, and more. I haven't spoken to her about married men. (*Is* Harvey married? I will believe, now, everything Agnieszka tells me, and most of what he tells her.) I haven't warned her about single or separated English men whose smiles are not easy, not relaxed. Let alone the ones whose smiles are too easy, too relaxed. I haven't warned her about cheap champagne in Hilton hotels, nor men playing three-card tricks, nor love. Unforgivably, my lack of sympathy for Harvey—my active dislike—has been conspicuous. Why couldn't I simply be happy for her, that she was happy?

I haven't taken care.

Agnieszka has gone to her room. One of Alan's office shirts lies on the ironing board, a creased arm dangling limply down.

SOMETIMES THE BATTER'S job is to score lots of runs as fast as he can, and sometimes it's to stay in and not get out and the runs are secondary. The bowler's priority is almost always to get the batter out but there are times when stopping the batter getting runs is the main thing.

God, this is a stupid game.

Agnieszka is proud, intelligent, ambitious, and she offers herself to an overweight buffoon who slouches over crosswords in the stale air of coffee bars. Selwyn— Selwyn is *gorgeous*, and if I were a fifteen-year-old girl I'd make sure he understands what that means—and he spends all day grumping about the injustice of the world. Me, I am married to a caring, conscientious man who rearranges cookery books by the light of the moon, and I rush away into the arms of man who wears yellow Wellington boots and whose job—and possibly whose life too, if I cared to investigate further—reeks of doom, disaster, things gone awry.

Stupid, stupid game. To decide who bats first, the umpires *toss a coin*. You can play the most brilliant game of your life and still end up on the losing side. You can be totally out of form and score zero and zero again and still prance with your team-mates in triumph at the end. And that's another thing: the spraying of champagne by the winners, the conspicuous waste. Fools. Champagne is for drinking, whether you win or lose. Just pass me the bottle.

I COME DOWN to the kitchen. The night of the long knives. The long, long night of the knives. The short knives, which so often get lost. And Selwyn will find them. Alan is sitting as before, in the one comfortable chair in the kitchen, with the cat on its arm. But in deeper darkness. Really, I cannot speak to an invisible man.

I switch on the small light over the cooker. 'Is that okay?'

It appears to be so. Indeed, Selwyn is safe, Agnieszka has not been raped, no rash crime of passion has been committed, no one has thrown him- or herself under a train. But it is not okay.

Alan knows. He knows where Selwyn is—Selwyn phoned him. He knows the loss-adjuster is my lover, and maybe has known ever since he first saw him that time in Edinburgh. He knows that Agnieszka is going through a difficult time, and probably even the details too, though I'm sure he doesn't want to. He knows pretty well everything. He may even have been to school with the three-card-trick man. If I ever did forget the loss-adjuster's phone number, all I'd have to do is ask him. He should be the umpire, not me.

I blink, and see Alan wearing that wide-brimmed white hat. He is tossing a coin. No, I want to tell him, there must be a better way, we need more time. But you only get so much time before the show moves on.

Unless I am pregnant. In which case there's a new member of the cast, a tiny loss-adjuster who's one quarter Spanish. Or a whole different show.

I have a sudden feeling of vertigo, as if I am high up on one of those cranes from which they take the aerial shots that show the players as just tiny white dots on the green field. I reach for a chair and sit down. Alan looks at me without expression. I breathe deeply, as I did with Agnieszka only minutes ago, and then I pull the chair closer to my book-rearranger, my knower of the alphabet and all the rules, this man without whom Selwyn would not have been. 'Alan, what are we going to do?'

He does that thing with his hands, linking and reversing them and pushing them out in front of him.

Then he says some obvious things, arranged in paragraphs and sub-sections, as if he's a committee, but they probably do need saying and he's by far the best person to say them. He says that this is surely not, vis-à-vis me and him and the loss-adjuster, an uncommon situation. In general. He actually does use that word, 'vis-à-vis.' He mentions Alex and Lyn, and Jamal and Sarah, and

Kirsten and Robin, he doesn't need to go on. So people have been through this before, are doing it all the time, and there are models, but that doesn't mean any one of those models is best for us. Assuming that the loss-adjuster and I love each other—

A tiny pause here, two commas instead of one, in case I want to interrupt. And I do want to interrupt: how dare he *assume* we love each other? Why can't I just have, what do they call it, a 'fling,' like everyone else? But instead, I go to the fridge to get some apple juice. There isn't any.

—we should probably separate. And Selwyn—

'Selwyn,' I say, coming back to the table. 'It's such an absurd name. It's for someone who's much older than sixteen. You should be called Selwyn and Selwyn should be Alan. No wonder he's confused and doesn't know what he wants. You know companies—big companies— spend millions of pounds on branding consultants and market research before they name a new product and we laugh at them but at least they're making an effort, putting a bit of thought into it. If you'd bought a pint for a deaf man down the pub and asked his advice you'd have done better than *Selwyn*.'

The fridge makes its fatuous grumbling noise, re-cooling.

Alan says that it wasn't like that at all and that I know it. Selwyn was the name of Annie's father and was the only name possible and was the right one, the name she needed her child to have—Annie, that is, Alan's first wife, whose own name has not been spoken in this kitchen for a very long time, who died of some awful illness when Selwyn was barely a year old and who was already ill at the time of his birth and knowing she was going to die. It's almost certainly true that I did know this before but any information I've ever had about Annie has been accidentally-on-purpose mislaid in some ancient and leaky storage device that can never be upgraded. A little bit because Annie was Alan's first and possibly only true love but mainly because illness is something I back away from, don't want to know about. It doesn't disgust me—I can clean up vomit, blood, shit, any other discharge the human body is capable of, as efficiently as the most seasoned and crusty nurse—but it does remind me: that I have only one inning, two if I'm lucky. Even colds, even glue ear.

Now Alan is telling me about sheep-farmers and a place in Wales that Annie's family came from, his throat and tongue negotiating the double ells with a noise that reminds me of when you push a clockwork toy that's stuck. He is also speaking, of course, in that premeditated voice, the one he uses to explain reverse spin, to explain anything or everything, the one that suggests he's concealing something. '*Yes, I know it's lipstick. It's there because Caroline—Caroline, you know? In human resources—she didn't get the promotion and she was pretty upset, in quite a state, falling all over the place, I had to take her down and get her a taxi . . .* ' But truly, I've never really believed there has been a Caroline. Though at times I might have wanted there to be, both for his own sake and for mine. And if he wasn't speaking in that voice he wouldn't be him. It's like that blockheadedness of Harvey that only makes Agnieszka fonder of him.

'Alan,' I say. 'I didn't mean to say that, about Selwyn's name. It just came out. What I meant was'—more double commas—'was that I love Selwyn as much as you do, as much as anyone *can* love him, and if we're going to talk about separating then we need to talk about exactly who gets separated from who and how and where and it's messy. It may be to you but to me the answer's not obvious.'

Alan thinks about this. Although it's possible he's thinking about the cookery books or something else entirely. 'By the way,' he says, 'I put the washing in. But I forgot the apron.'

I look towards the back of the door where the apron

is hanging, a thin black winding sheet, both stripes and stains invisible in this murk we're sitting in. In this bad light. 'Next time,' I say.

Alan is stroking the cat, which is still sitting on the arm of his chair, listening in. Stroking quite hard, obsessively, though he's probably no longer aware he's doing it, and because the cat is moulting, by now there's a loose ball of cat-hairs at the base of its spine, at the end of Alan's stroke. I make a bowl shape with my hands and offer it to him. He picks up the cat-hairs and drops them into my hands. I've no idea what it means but this is the most imaginative and intimate thing we've done together for ten years.

BOREDOM, SKILL, PLAY, work. You knead or stir and bring a finger or spoon to your tongue to check the seasoning, and if a pencil sharpener accidentally gets swept into the mix it should still turn out all right. But sometimes even for the experts it is hard not to let one taste—desire; duty—overwhelm the others.

I go to Selwyn's room and lie down on his bed and think of him walking away from me along the pavement to the loss-adjuster's flat—he didn't turn to look back, it was I who did that—and I look for my phone and call a cab.

*M*esopotamia is now Iraq. On the seat, in the cab on my way to the loss-adjuster's, there are some pages from yesterday's newspaper. Not the cricket, thank God, but the inside pages, where I read about an Iraqi man who took his wife, who had been housebound for three weeks, out to the market for an ice cream. As they passed some children playing football on a patch of waste ground two cars drew up and men took guns from the boots of the cars and shot the children. The men got back in their cars and drove off, leaving the children dead or dying on the ground. The onlookers, witnesses, those who stood by, rather than go to help the children, rushed home, got their own guns, and began firing—Sunnis at Shias, Shias at Sunnis. Only when their ammunition was running out, about a couple of hours later, did they start picking up the children.

I feel loose, hollowed out, sick. I rest my head against the cab window. The traffic at this hour is light but there are still people on the pavements, walking, waiting, arguing, flirting, making decisions. *Buy one, get one free* announces a sticker in a shop window. *Other colors and designs available—please ask inside.*

I HAVE A key. The loss-adjuster is awake when I arrive. Without me, he has no cause for early nights. He is reading.

Selwyn is asleep on the sofa, under a duvet, and the loss-adjuster is sitting in the armchair, his book in his lap. This room I have come into is a remote place I might have invented, but not these two people in it. I sit on the floor, my back against the chair, my head against the loss-adjuster's leg.

He carries on reading, aloud. It isn't Dickens or Aristotle, nor is it a book about some wizened, *Wisden*-ed cricketer.

'If, while travelling, the countryside possesses any significance at all for you, then going from Russia to Siberia you could have a very boring time from the Urals right up to the Yenisey. The chilly plain, the twisted birch-trees, the pools, the occasional islands, snow in May and the barren, bleak banks of the tributaries of the Ob . . . '

Selwyn stirs on the sofa, scrunches up. The fetal position. Sound travels—I've read this, and believe it—into the womb: Mozart, traffic noise, a book being read aloud.

I feel safe here. I am on the right road. The only wind is the loss-adjuster's voice. I begin to untie his shoelaces.

'There is little space between the banks of the Yenisey. The low billows strive to outstrip each other, jostle each other, form spirals, and it seems odd that this Hercules has not yet washed the banks away and drilled a hole through the bottom . . . '

I have nothing, now, to say. I have stopped thinking.

'The power and enchantment of the taiga lie not in titanic trees or the silence of the graveyard, but in the fact that only birds of passage know where it ends. Over the first twenty-four hours you pay no attention to it; on the second and third you are full of wonderment, and by the fourth and fifth you are experiencing the sensation that you will never manage to emerge from this green monster . . . '

I rub my face against his trouser legs and look up at his lips, their tiny indefatigable movement along the path of words. Down here on the forest floor, beneath the canopy of branches, the air is damp and breathy.

'According to the tales of the coachmen, in the taiga live

bears, wolves, elks, sable and wild goats. When there is no
work at home the countrymen living along the highway spend
whole weeks in the taiga shooting game. The art of the hunter
here is very simple: if the gun goes off—thank God; but if it
misfires—do not ask the bear for mercy . . . '

Not mercy, no, it's not mercy I want or am asking
for, though I can see that if Selwyn woke he might decide
that's what I'm doing, kneeling before this man's feet to
remove his shoes, moving up and further in to usurp that
book.

Which surrenders unconditionally.

And before I know it I'm on the bed and the bear is
upon me and I'm lashing out, biting, punching, beating
him off and pulling him into me as hard and deep as I
can. Before I know it I'm riding him, bucking, gripping
hard on the folds round his neck, behind his arm-pits,
the flab on his hips, sweating, thrashing, slabbering,
grunting, bleeding from cuts and from scratches, being
knocked against the trees. Because this has to be *first*, and
if it isn't then I have to make it so. Before any knowledge
at all, before any rules or white lines or the barest inkling
of what is or is not fair play.

THE LAWS OF cricket were codified in 1744, Selwyn
once told me, at the tag end of a Googling session. I was

emptying shopping bags at the time, putting a cereal packet on the shelf. The eighteenth century again: they hanged people for stealing a loaf of bread, and they wrote down the laws of cricket, and women who read books wore blue stockings. Me, I have been alive only since the end of the 1960s. So many things I have not noticed, taken account of, that have been here around me for much longer than me, a way of putting it that doesn't quite make sense. And yet I noticed, and have remembered, that.

And the time I mentioned Franco and Selwyn thought I was talking about the man who runs the cap-puccino place down the road, and then someone from *Big Brother*, and then some boy singer who only eleven-year-olds and mothers could possibly be interested in. He seriously had no idea who Franco—*the* Franco—was. He was about twelve, he was becoming curious and had come down to the kitchen for something to eat or to see what kind of game Alan and I were playing. (Alan was once amazed that I'd never heard of Sir Alec Douglas-Home, and had only the vaguest idea about Jim Callaghan, but that's, somehow, different.)

The period before we come on the scene—all that time, for instance, in our parents' lives before *us*, before they even knew each other, what *can* they have been doing?—is dead ground. We can't see it from the window we're looking out from; we have to go up in a helicopter, or creep out of the house at night. But things grow there. Weeds. Shrubs. Strange little hardy flowers.

Selwyn's phone calls to Alan—those grew there, in the dead ground before I arrived. Small, deep purple flowers on long stems, growing in the crack between the pavement and a wall, footsteps going by, oblivious. Between the time Annie died and the time I arrived, when Selwyn was five, there was just Alan and Selwyn. A few Agnieszkas and Brancas and Tatijanas passing through, but just the two constants, and between them something must have pollinated. Then I came along and Selwyn and I looked at each other and sprouted all kinds of gaudy blooms, but there was still that other plant, still is.

So whose team is he on? This boy who so wants me at home yet turns on the pavement and walks away. Whose team am *I* on? This is not, surely, an unprecedented example of human behavior. Somewhere in the journals there must be a word to describe it, that encompasses these matters—the batsman who heads back to the pavilion even though the umpire has not given him out; or, conversely, who refuses to leave the pitch after he's been clean bowled; the bowler who keeps on bowling after his over is over; the fielder who picks up the ball and, rather than throwing it back to the wicket-keeper, tosses it into the crowd—a word coined by an Austrian psychoanalyst or an Australian cricket correspondent.

'How do you spell that?'

'Dombrowski. It's not hard.'

The big woman at the desk turns pages in a box file, running her finger down lists, while answering the phone with her other hand and somehow also managing to wave to someone going out of the door behind me. It is these women—immovable, Ganesha-like, with four hands and enormous ears and placid eyes—who hold these places together, who stop them flying apart to the ends of the earth.

I have come to Agnieszka's college to speak with her, because it cannot wait—to tell her how sorry I am that I have not paid attention, how grateful I am to her for arranging the cricket game on Sunday, which was something she did only and without one jot of self-interest to divert and perhaps amuse me and make me more gentle. I am already late. I am always late, and always impatient, things that make no sense together, that shouldn't even belong in the same sentence. This is what happens, I think, in the second innings.

Agnieszka is in a class, the big woman tells me, at the

same time as changing another student's course from hairdressing to hospitality management on her computer screen and ordering more paper for the photocopier. She will be out in twenty minutes.

I turn to the notice-board, the rooms to rent for non-smokers and the DVD-players for sale and the drummers needed, and then see through a glass door a room with chairs and tables. I go into this room and sit down on a sofa beside a low table littered with sandwich wrappers. It's far too warm in here, the air stale and clammy, but as I look to see if there's a window that can be opened I become aware that I've been asked a question.

In front of me there's a boy who in some ways is like a younger version of Selwyn—pink cheeks, and no sign that he's started to shave—but in other ways not at all: he's neat, he wears glasses, he doesn't know the meaning of doubt and all his grades are A.

'Coffee?'

I must have smiled because he's putting money into a machine and bringing me something brown and hot in a paper cup.

'No, really, you shouldn't,' I say, taking the scalding cup from his hands and reaching quickly for the table, and he shrugs and tells me it's nothing, it's cheap, and I immediately realize I am in the room Agnieszka calls the bar, the room where Harvey sits. This very sofa.

The boy sits down opposite me. He has mistaken me for another student, or perhaps a teacher—but this is not a mistake, I *am* a teacher. The invention of vulcanized rubber, the hydrogen balloon. And I am completely familiar with this clammy air, and with these lovely strangers who move around me in their outer-space clothes, with their tattoos in unexpected places and their seething hormones and their gangly legs that will not fit under the table. Dutch, Chinese, other Poles, and the bashful or grumpy English. Bears, wolves, elk, sable and wild goat.

Not one of them, I realize, has any interest in cricket. They are too carefree, or knotted. It is not on their syllabus.

England began today at 24 for 3—these are numbers that for no logical reason have stuck in my head, like those numbers from Selwyn's website, the eight spiders and the eleven-year-old pope (for whom they would have had to have made a special child-sized crown, or whatever does go on a pope's head). If they score another 263 runs, they will win; if seven of their batters get out, they will lose; if they play each ball just to stay alive and not die the game will have been for nothing, except pride.

The boy wearing glasses is speaking to me: 'So after

two years I will be earning . . . ' But there is Agnieszka at the door, her face oddly blank, showing no surprise to see me here.

'O Agnieszka'—the vocative, it just comes out, as if this college teaches Latin. And then nothing, because there is so much. 'Agnieszka, please, I'm so sorry—'

She sits beside me on the sofa. A man with a stubbly beard moves his cycling helmet to let her in. She is not happy at all, and nothing I had intended to say will make her so. She has been with Harvey to visit his mother.

'She is so small,' she says. 'Like a baby, but her hair is white. And she never . . . ' Agnieszka flutters her eyelids.

'She doesn't have a man?'

'No, not like that.' She closes one eye, then opens it and closes the other.

We stare at each other until I have to force myself not to look away, because Agnieszka is so much stronger, prettier, more vulnerable and more intelligent than I've allowed her to be. 'Ah,' I say. 'She doesn't *blink*?'

Agnieszka nods vigorously. She blinks at me quickly, with both eyes, and I blink back and we grin. Then she becomes serious, because she is trying to describe to me something which clearly was very strange to her. It seems that the mother led her around the house and showed her a lot of brand-new and expensive objects: the TV, of course, but then a camera, and a case of champagne, and a statue of a fish that flies—'A dolphin?' 'Yes, doll-fish'—and in the kitchen some complicated gadgets which I can only assume, from Agnieszka's descriptions, must have been a blender and an espresso machine, or possibly an ice-cream maker.

'Like a shop,' says Agnieszka. 'Like Harold's.'

'Harrods.'

'Yes, like Harold's. And then Harvey, he takes me to his mother's desk and he shows me some papers and he explains what is this.' She takes an envelope from her bag and offers it to me. Inside is a voucher for two people to stay in a time-share apartment in Spain for two weeks in November.

I begin to understand. 'So she's *won* all these things?'

'Yes, yes!' says Agnieszka. 'They are prizes. She does competitions. I tell this to Harvey, and he says no, she *wins* competitions.'

'Well, *someone's* got to win them,' I say. I don't mean to be this enthusiastic. Someone with the patience to cut out the side panels from cereal packets with all their virtues randomly listed and renumber them in the only correct order and fill in the dotted line after 'I buy this stuff because . . . ' Because, because, because—always the right reason, and never in more than ten words. *I like sex with the loss-adjuster because* . . . But this does explain the pen, the deep-sea diver's watch, the tickets to the musical, the vouchers for the hotel. The lifetime's supply of cans of soup. The crosswords. Jingles, I'm thinking, riddles, anagrams, acrostics, and how impossibly beyond this good Polish girl's experience all this must be, but she hasn't finished yet.

'Harvey,' she says. 'He is sitting . . . ' She shoos the man with cycling helmet off the end of the sofa—he doesn't stand a chance, in the face of her need he is putty—and scrunches herself up like she's inside a cardboard box. She holds this pose for a long time, as if we are playing charades and I must guess the answer, the title of a film, or a book. But I cannot guess.

The boy with glasses and pink cheeks, the boy who knows no doubt and might even be able to help me here, has vanished. Already he will be earning more than me.

'So I say to this mother, him too?' Agnieszka is sitting up again, but looks as if she'd prefer to be still inside a box. 'She smiles at me like we are speaking about some private thing—you know, woman thing, not for men—and she says, a newspaper for children, many years before. She goes to her desk, she shows me. The pages are yellow. With pictures, and words in bubbles coming out of their mouths—'

'Cartoons.'

'—and she promises to look after him and the priest, he signs.'

'The priest?'

'Or lawyer, she says. Or teacher or magistrate. What is magistrate?'

I'm not terribly sure. 'A judge,' I say. 'In a court of law.' A kind of umpire, but sitting down.

'But priest is best, she says.'

'I doubt that very much.'

'And Harvey, now he has gone to the toilet, he does not like this talking.'

'No.' I've said this before but now I mean it. This is a horrible, horrible story. 'Agnieszka, are you sure you've got this right? You're saying that Harvey's mother won him in a competition? That he was the prize?' This must be a mistake, a mistranslation from Agnieszka's Polish understanding of what she has been through.

She ignores me. I am dim, thick, pea-brained.

'We wait. Long time. No man can piss this long, really, I know this. His mother, she says nothing, I hear in the kitchen the fridge making noise—'

I know that noise. Only last night. A rattling, like its

stomach is churning, as if it had a body and even a soul, which it doesn't. It's pathetic.

'—so I go to the toilet door and listen, then his mother comes too and she bangs on the door very loud and Harvey shouts to us go away, go away, and I am thinking is he speaking to his mother or to me, this silly boy.'

She looks at me, as if I'm still supposed to know the answer and it's obvious, I'm just pretending to be stupid. The title of a film, or a book.

The chilly plain, the twisted birch-trees, the pools, the occasional islands, snow in May and the barren, bleak banks of the tributaries of the Ob . . .

Bad light. Bad light. Bad light.

Heads or tails?

Heads.

She starts to cry.

I let her. Selwyn did not cry, I did not cry, and it needs to be done. And somehow she needs me to be with her, in this public room with its stew of indifference and mildly curious stares, so she can do this. So let her. For however long.

THERE WILL BE a time, if I want there to be a time, when Alan and I will be sitting comfortably together on the sofa watching men dressed in white play cricket on TV. That man's already had his turn at bowling, I will be thinking. It must be someone else's turn now.

Why do they get runs for that? The batter didn't even hit the ball.

And then: 'But the fielder caught it, I saw him—why's the batter still there, why's he not out?'

Alan will look at me. Perhaps he *has* explained this to me before, and I've forgotten. I'm trying, I have been trying, I will be trying. It was not a stupid question.

He will still be looking at me. He is being patient, but needs me to know that he is being patient, that I am a person he has to be patient with.

'No ball,' he will say. And then will quietly elucidate the rule about the bowler's front foot and where it must or mustn't be when he releases the ball. Again the deliberate voice, and again, although it serves no purpose and I have no good reason to entertain it, I will have the nagging suspicion that he is making all this up as he goes along; that everything he has told me so far is a fairy tale, or an ingenious parody or piece of satire; that he is deliberately misleading me or testing me for some purpose I cannot guess.

Though I never doubted him, as I never doubted the loss-adjuster, when he told me that he loved me.

Explain, please. Even if it changes nothing. And don't tell me that you haven't got the time, or that I can only learn it by doing it, even though both may be true.

ANOTHER SOFA.

I am walking away from Agnieszka's college and towards the Tube station where the gypsy does his trick, which is not the nearest Tube station but I feel a need just now to see that man, even if only to know that he is still there; and besides, I have no money. I have left my handbag in the college, among the sports bags and paper cups and take-away cartons in the room they call a bar, or in the loss-adjuster's car, when he drove me to the college, or perhaps even before that, in his flat. How easy it is, when you're not trying, to cast yourself adrift.

It will be a long walk. There are hours left in the day. I have passed an Italian restaurant where a man and woman were sitting at a table eating spaghetti—skillfully, politely, not dribbling it down their chins, and in silence. And now I pause in front of a shop selling sofas where another couple—young, late twenties—are trying out the chairs and sofas displayed in the front window. He sits in an armchair, stretches out his legs. She watches, arms folded, then sits at one end of a sofa. He joins her. Without a TV in front of them they're at a loss; both look sideways, behind, at other models. She gets up and goes over to the chair he was sitting in before, runs her hand along the fabric. The salesman hovers, deferential, attempting to deduce which one of them makes the decisions, which one of them pays. This furniture is expensive; it is an investment, intended to last many years.

You could do a game-show like this: have couples choosing sofas, and the audience has to predict which couple will stay together longest. It might seem obvious—moving and speaking as one, as against tripping over each other's words and feet—but in fact often I think they'd get it wrong.

My mobile rings, in my pocket. I had thought it was in my handbag.

The loss-adjuster, who never phones, has my bag, which I never lose.

This is barely a conversation.

'We were going on a journey,' he adds.

'We were?'

'You remember. *If, while travelling, the countryside possesses any significance at all for you . . .* '

'The countryside? No.'

'Not the English countryside.'

'I know. It's a translation.'

'I love you.'

'Yes. I've never . . . This journey—where's he going to?'

'Siberia. A prison camp.'

I laugh. It's not exactly a bed of roses.

We could talk about Selwyn, but that would be unfair, to use him as a distraction. There is a long silence in which I can hear the loss-adjuster's breathing, and feel it too, on my skin. Inside the shop the woman is walking towards the door, the man following, glancing back at the sofa. The salesman is looking directly towards me, a sour expression on his face, as if it's entirely my fault he hasn't made a sale. And then I tell the loss-adjuster to skip to the end and read the description of the prison camp—the freezing cold, the bare wooden huts, the slop buckets, the brutish guards who deal out punishments on a whim—and I say I could be happy there, with him.

I WALK ON, beneath a sky that earlier was clear but now has clouds in it, bumping each other along. It will rain, perhaps. Is there enough moisture in the air to make the ball swing, if that's what moisture does? God knows.

Certainly the experts don't. Or at least, they differ—sitting safe in the studio, paid their flat fee whether they get it right or not, dispensing predictions and advice in their solemn or eager voices. Bell is seeing the ball well today, they say, he looks to have settled in for a big score—and next ball he's clean bowled. And then the horrible wisdom of hindsight—he should never have played that shot, he should have waited for the next over—which isn't wisdom at all. Besides, how can anyone trust a man who wears a red-and-yellow tie with a pink shirt?

Pace yourself, they say. Build your innings by stages—ten runs, and then the next ten runs, don't try to win the match in one day.

I have never been good at taking advice. I listen, and it all sounds sensible, but then I realize they're talking to *me* and it makes no sense at all, it bears no relation to life as I am experiencing it, which is a kind of quivering chaos shot through with threads of baffling significance.

There are some days, I admit, which are so perfect they seem to have been composed by Scarlatti; but many more days that are written by a monkey at a typewriter. And there are odd days when, just going about my normal routine, I notice an abnormally high number of pregnant women, or people wearing new shoes. Today it is the turn of tramps and beggars: three of them—no: five, six—between the sofa shop and the Tube station. Their begging technique is useless (surely someone should offer training?): they mumble, they don't make eye contact. They are bulked out with layers of ancient clothes. I think they are retired umpires down on their luck, still encumbered with the cast-off jumpers of bowlers who have worked up a sweat and then forgotten to retrieve them. Or perhaps they've made one too many bad decisions, and they've been sacked.

Without umpires, where would bowlers hang their hats and jumpers? They'd simply drop them to the ground, like Selwyn does around the house: school tie on the draining board, jeans on the stairs, boxers and socks in the shower room. I bend and gather, bend and gather, like a reaper in a painting by Millet.

Enforcing discipline: another thing I have never been good at.

But no one could call me lazy. If a batsman scores a hundred runs and scoots the length of the cricket pitch for every one of them he will have run—wait—about one and a quarter miles. Not much, considering—I mean, considering that sometimes they just smash the ball out of the field and don't bother to run at all, and they have breaks for lunch and tea, and if they time it well they get a night's sleep halfway through. Me, I have scored at least a double century today, more than Mithali Raj, while no one was looking, and every one of those runs I have walked.

When I get to the Tube station my legs shut down, their job done. To those moving around me, who find my stillness an obstruction, I must look like a tourist, lost. I am not a tourist, I live here; and I am not lost, I am simply taking account of—*basking in*—this pause before I pass through the barrier and go down the escalator to one of the two platforms. A man in a tearing hurry bashes my elbow with his laptop bag as he grabs an *Evening Standard*, fumbles for change and then turns to the back page: England were 107 for 5 at lunch. I become aware that someone's watching me, and I know before I look round it's the card-man, the gypsy, standing with his big hands by his upturned box.

He's alone, without his stooge who wears glasses and brings in the punters. There's something we have in common, this man and I, and I think I recognize what it is: he too is a person for whom Sunday-night TV plays are as alien a phenomenon as Korean folk dancing. There's a code the characters speak in (most of the lines—the actors also—are from other TV plays, slightly rearranged) that excludes us; and they seem to beat each other up and have sex in the same strange code. We are baffled by the way these plays are at once both implausible (for me) and predictable (for Alan, who has worked out who the murderer is within the first half hour). Some might say the same about cricket, but at least cricket doesn't pretend to be *realistic*.

The card-man steps forward and offers me the three cards, slightly grubby. Although I know I would win, that I could touch with my finger the queen of spades even if I stood blindfold while he shuffled the cards like a concert pianist performing some show-off virtuoso piece, I decline. Instead, I ask him a question you might ask someone you've known for years, and who knows you better than you do yourself. 'Can you lend me some money?'

From inside his jacket he takes a wad of notes, more hard cash than I have ever seen in any man's or woman's hand. This is real money, not some flimsy bit of plastic: enough to put Selwyn through college, enough to replace Mr Chidambaram's entire stock of fashion fabrics. He peels off five twenty-pound notes. I shake my head. He gives me two five-pound notes and puts the rest back in his pocket before I can refuse again.

We look at each other, not as if we're waiting for something to be said but then he speaks anyway. He tells me they've just come back on the field after tea at 199 for 7. 'Eighty-eight more runs to win, three wickets to lose,' he says, in his deadpan voice that tells things how they are.

I turn and enter the Tube station. A poster warns me

to be careful on the escalator: last year there were thirty-nine injuries, two fatalities. These insistent, random, exact numbers. The twelve newborn children being given each day to the wrong parents (although who is to say they are wrong?). Selwyn, shouting at me from his computer screen his distracting but compelling facts: 'Mum, get this.' A goldfish kept in a dark room will turn white. A polar bear's skin is black. The youngest pope was eleven. If you are stuck in quicksand, lie back, spread yourself wide, and raise your legs slowly. On average, left-handed people die nine years earlier than right-handed people.

But the loss-adjuster is not average.

SOMEWHERE IN THE south of England a sixteen-year-old boy playing for his school Second Eleven waits for the ball to come on to him, takes half a step back and with a last-second swivel of his wrists sends the ball speeding over the grass between two fielders; and he knows, this boy, he just *knows* that however many more matches he will play, however many years he will live, never again will he hit the ball with such sweet precision. On a parched and dusty maidan in the outskirts of Karachi a nine-year-old boy spins the balls towards his older brother's friend, whose arm-locks are vicious and painful; the ball floats in the air long enough for the older boy to stride forwards and grin in anticipation before missing it completely. In the nets of a junior academy in Perth, Western Australia, a man places a coin on the spot where a seventeen-year-old bowler must pitch the ball, and the boy walks solemnly back to the start of his run-up. On a gritty sloping road in Kenya a long-legged boy sprints downhill after the bouncing ball, swerves in mid-air to avoid a motorbike, falls headlong on the ground and comes up with the ball in his hand and blood streaming from his elbows and knees. On a beach in Kingston, Jamaica; in an alleyway in Ahmadabad, with a broom handle used as a bat; in the basement of a multi-storey car park in Hunslet, West Yorkshire, while the rain teems down outside; in a back yard in Johannesburg, against a wicket chalked on a breezeblock wall. Sometimes sisters may be allowed to field but generally what I see is a boy, a boy, a boy, a boy. In a corridor overlooking the maidan in Karachi a girl carrying a tray of food—bread, tea, cakes, I can only imagine—pauses at a window to watch the young spinner's next ball. Her face comes only just above the bottom of the window frame. From somewhere further inside the building an impatient voice calls out her name, and she turns and is gone.

THE LOSS-ADJUSTER'S SMILE is not sheepish. It's goatish.

I want them both, the sheep and the goats, and if I can't have them then a way has to be invented. It's called civilisation, the progress of.

A Hundred-and-One Great Inventions.

I want to be this batter, and that bowler, not either/or, and right now I have easily enough strength to do this. An *all-rounder*, yes, and more than that: an all-rounder who can play for both teams. I don't care who's umpire but I trust the dark-skinned man more than the other one. He has something Mesopotamian, Sumerian, about his features. Something aquiline.

He shakes his head.

Actually he doesn't even do that: he just tilts his head sideways and slightly upwards, as if some unidentifiable smell has just wafted within range of his nostrils, or as if Agnieszka has asked a question about seagulls, or—more precisely—as if the bowler has just flung his arms up in the air and appealed in a voice of 150 decibels for a wicket. The answer is no. The answer is that the question isn't even worth considering.

We are grown-ups here. We are not children in the park. No one can play for both sides, that's not how it works.

I am down, now, at the level of choosing, between the platforms. A train rushes in: the noise of its approach drowning out words, and the air it displaces rushing against my face—grit in my eyes, my hair all to pieces. It's full, and I let it pass. As the doors are closing an Indian woman wriggles her way in, pressing against a Chinese couple who in turn are squeezed against an Englishman who is trying to read a book. This is the same in all languages and really it has nothing to do with choosing, not now; it is about knowledge, and consciousness. I'm completely relaxed. The body—which is never just flesh, but is that first of all—knows. It's not just an envelope for a clever letter, explaining things. It seeks—to be stretched, tested, to score runs off the fastest or most awkward delivery that's sent towards it: intelligent play, the best it can do. I live in it; I trust it. It is spiced best with desire.

Another carriage halts in front of me and I step in, ridiculously happy to be without my handbag—I have nothing to guard, I am free. The train gathers speed, carrying me towards the loss-adjuster's flat. Selwyn may already be there, before me, or he may not.

Oddly, for someone who is such a defensive driver, for someone who has said sorry so often and stood aside to let a stranger past—I could go on: for someone who has always (usually) been happy to share; someone who's more interested in the view than where she's going to; someone who almost never ticks the 'strongly agree' or 'strongly disagree' boxes; someone who never ticks boxes at all because there must be something more interesting to do than tick boxes, even if it's just staring out of the window; someone who always assumes that she'll be doing the washing up, even when it's not her turn; someone who is always among the last to be picked, because she's easily distracted and lacks what they call the killer instinct; someone who thinks of herself as someone who's not bothered about winning—oddly, then, as I say, I don't want to play for a draw, I want to win. But it doesn't feel odd.

What it does feel is good, if a bit dark, even though it probably isn't, outside. Just more clouds. External factors: age, income, prospects, dependants. The game will still be going on, heading towards whatever will be its conclusion, and the umpires, the big burly one with the wedding hat and the small dark one, will be still standing in the field like statues. Now the burly one is walking over to the dark one and they are whispering together. Conferring, is the word used. Everyone else is quiet, as if they are trying to overhear what is being said, but they can't. The burly one has a meeting arranged with a woman at seven-thirty and he really wants to get this game wrapped up, over and done. The woman once won a singing competition on a TV show and the pearls she wears are real. This is unlikely but true. Together, the umpires look up at the clouds, seeking guidance from on high. If they offer me the light I will not take it.